IN THE BOARDROOM

Greek tycoons become devoted dads!

The Andreas brothers were born with success in their blood.... Hardworking and at the top of their game, they're all-about-the-money kind of guys who think business, not babies. That is, until now!

Because when babies arrive in the boardroom, work is going to be the last thing on the minds of these tycoons!

Don't miss any of the fabulous stories in Susan Meier's brand-new trilogy:

The Baby Project—April 2011
Second Chance Baby—May 2011
Baby on the Ranch—June 2011

Dear Reader,

The cast of characters for the Babies in the Boardroom trilogy was determined when I wrote book one, *The Baby Project*. But imagine my surprise when I began hammering out chapter one of book two, *Second Chance Baby*, and I discovered that the heroine, Nick Andreas's ex-wife, was pregnant.

A million questions popped into my head. Who is the father? Is she married? What's going on here? Worse… how is Nick going to handle this?

Sometimes writing a book is like that. The characters get minds of their own about how they want their stories to go and Maggie wasn't the kind to sit around waiting for Nick to show up in her life again. She'd gotten married, gotten pregnant and then discovered her husband had been cheating on her.

Nick and Maggie were two of the most fun, most romantic characters I've ever created. Maggie just sweeps you away with her absolute determination to be the person everyone can lean on, when she's the person who could use a little help herself.

Turn the page and step into a fun, heartwarming story about a love that certainly deserves a second chance, if the characters can get beyond their past hurts and heal.

Susan Meier

P.S. Look for Cade's story, *Baby on the Ranch*, coming soon!

SUSAN MEIER

Second Chance Baby

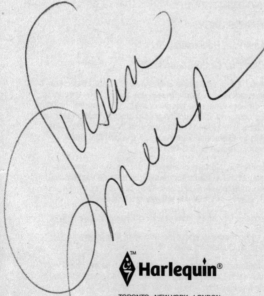

™
Harlequin®

TORONTO NEW YORK LONDON
AMSTERDAM PARIS SYDNEY HAMBURG
STOCKHOLM ATHENS TOKYO MILAN MADRID
PRAGUE WARSAW BUDAPEST AUCKLAND

Recycling programs
for this product may
not exist in your area.

ISBN-13: 978-0-373-17727-1

SECOND CHANCE BABY

First North American Publication 2011

Susan Meier spent most of her twenties thinking she was a job-hopper—until she began to write and realized everything that had come before was only research! One of eleven children, with twenty-four nieces and nephews and three kids of her own, Susan has had plenty of real-life experience watching romance blossom in unexpected ways. She lives in western Pennsylvania with her wonderful husband, Mike, three children and two overfed, well-cuddled cats, Sophie and Fluffy. You can visit Susan's website at www.susanmeier.com.

CHAPTER ONE

"Your ex-wife applied for the job as your assistant."

Nick Andreas glanced up at his current assistant, soon-to-be-retired Julie Farnsworth. He'd just flown back to North Carolina after six weeks in New York City. He was exhausted and wanted nothing more than to go to his beach house, get out of his monkey suit and take a nap on his hammock. He'd only popped into the office because he had a huge bid due to renew the government contract that was the bread and butter of his manufacturing plant. He had to get an assistant in now.

He just wasn't sure hiring Maggie Forsythe as Julie's replacement was the best way to go. When he had a bid due, his assistant worked with him—*directly with him, at his side*—ten hours a day, six days a week. No man wanted to spend that much time with his ex-wife. Not even an ex-wife he hadn't seen in fifteen years. An ex-wife he barely remembered.

He tossed his pen to his desk. "You wouldn't be telling me this if she wasn't qualified."

"She's qualified. Overqualified in some respects."

"And she actually applied?"

"Well, we certainly didn't drag her in off the street."

He laughed and leaned back in his chair. So Maggie wanted to work for him? He smiled skeptically as weird feelings assaulted him. He hadn't thought about Maggie Forsythe in over a decade. Now, suddenly, he could vividly recall how the sun would catch her red hair and make it sparkle, her wide, happy smile, the sound of her laughter.

"Sorry if I'm finding all this a little hard to believe, but we didn't exactly part on the best of terms. Andreas Manufacturing should be the last place she wants to work."

His sixty-five-year-old assistant caught his gaze with serious dark eyes. "She needs the money."

She was broke? The way he'd been when they'd met?

Memories of his childhood and teen years cascaded through his brain like water spilling from a waterfall. Maggie at six, toothless in first grade, dividing her morning snack with him before they went into the building so no one in their class would see he hadn't brought one. Maggie at twelve, fishing with him so he and his mom could have something for supper. Maggie at sixteen, hanging out in the souvenir shop where he worked, entertaining him on long, boring afternoons before the tourist season picked up. Maggie at eighteen, swollen with his child.

A long-forgotten ache filled his chest and made him scowl. The woman he was remembering with such fondness had dropped him like a hot potato when she'd lost their baby. She hadn't loved him. She'd only married him because he'd gotten her pregnant one reckless night. Twenty minutes after they'd returned from the hospital after her miscarriage, she'd been out the door of his mom's house. Out of his life.

"She should have as many reservations about with me as I have about working with her."

"Her stepmom died while you were in Nev has it, she came home for the funeral and dec needed her. She quit her job and moved back permanently but in three weeks of looking she couldn't find work—unless she wants to commute to the city." Julie peered at him over the rim of her glasses. "Aside from tourism, you're the only real employer in Ocean Palms."

He picked up his pen again. "Hire her."

Julie gasped softly. "Really?"

"Sure. We were married as kids. Fifteen years have gone by." He wasn't such a selfish, self-centered oaf that he'd let someone suffer because she had the misfortune of having a history with him. He knew what it was like to have no options. He'd spent his entire childhood living hand-to-mouth. He wouldn't ignore the person who, as a child, had shared with him, helped him, even rescued him a time or two.

Plus, if Julie said Maggie was the person for the job then she was.

Julie rose. "Okay. She's in my office. She said she can begin today. I'll bring her in and we can get started."

Nick sat up in his seat. Today? He didn't even have ten minutes to mentally prepare?

Julie walked to his office door and opened it. "Come in, Maggie."

A true Southern gentleman, Nick rose from the tall-back chair behind his huge mahogany desk. Ridiculously, he couldn't squelch the pride that surged up in him as he took in the expensive Persian rugs that sat on the hardwood floors of his office, the lamps from China, the heavy leather sofa and chair in the conversation area, the art from the broker in New York City. He was rich, successful, and his office showed it. He'd fulfilled the promise of his youth. He had brains and skill and he'd parlayed those into wealth beyond anyone's expectations. One look at his office would tell Maggie he wasn't the eighteen-year-old boy she'd deserted anymore.

The click of high heels on the hardwood announced her arrival two seconds before she appeared in his doorway. Her gorgeous red hair flowed around her, but it was shaped and curled in a way that framed her face, not straight as she had worn it when they were married. Her once sparkly green eyes now held soul-searching intensity. Her full red lips rose slightly in a reluctant smile.

Just as he wasn't the eighteen-year-old she'd left behind anymore, she didn't look a thing like his Maggie.

He relaxed as his gaze involuntarily fell from her face to her dress. A simple red tank dress that showed off a newly acquired suntan, but also couldn't hide her slightly protruding stomach.

She was pregnant?

He gave her tummy a more thorough scrutiny.

She was pregnant.

And suddenly he *was* that eighteen-year-old boy again. Seeing his woman, the love of his life, swollen with his child. More memories washed over him. The dreams he'd had for the kind of father he would be rose up as if he'd been lost in them only yesterday. Love for her, the woman bearing his child, burst in his chest.

But this wasn't his child. She'd lost their child.

And she didn't love him.

Hell, he no longer loved her.

"Come in," he said. His voice was tight with a bit of a squeak but he ignored that, motioning to the chair in front of his desk.

Maggie took a few hesitant steps inside. Now trim instead of lanky, she wore her pregnancy the same way another woman would wear a designer dress.

That was when he realized she was probably married.

Happily married. Not scared and hesitant, with no other options because her stepmom had kicked her out of the house. But happy. Having a child with the man she loved.

He swallowed the knot that formed in his throat, reminding himself that these emotions churning through him were ridiculous. He was over her. Plus, they hadn't even seen each other in fifteen years. The feelings weren't really feelings. They were residue. Like cobwebs that had clung to the walls of his brain and would disappear once he got to know the adult Maggie.

"Julie wants to hire you but I have a few reservations."

He didn't even try to stop the words that flowed from his mouth. Though he'd already told Julie to hire her, now that he saw she was pregnant, he had some concerns. Not about the "feelings" seeing her pregnant aroused, but about her ability to do the job.

She gracefully sat on the chair in front of his desk, smiled softly. "You mean because we were once married?"

He snorted a laugh, but Julie's hand flew to her throat. "You know, I think I'll just go get us some coffee."

Nick said, "She can't drink coffee," at the same time that Maggie said, "I don't drink coffee."

Julie said, "Then I'll get some coffee for myself." She fled the room, closing the door behind her.

Nick sat back in his chair, reaching deep inside himself for the calm that was his trademark. He had to treat her as any other employee and speak accordingly.

"For the next four weeks I need my assistant to work ten-hour days."

"Six days a week. I get that. Julie told me."

"Can you keep up?"

"Of course I can keep up. I'm pregnant not sick."

The room plunged into eerie silence. Memories of

the day she'd lost their baby haunted him like menacing ghosts.

As if recognizing where his thoughts had gone, Maggie sighed. "Nick, I'm fine. Really. And I need this job. If you don't hire me I'll have to get work in the city and commute an hour each way."

"An hour commute might be better for a pregnant woman than racing around the plant looking for documents I need, assembling information from different departments—"

He paused to catch her gaze and when he saw green eyes sparking with fire, everything he intended to say fell out of his head. He remembered that look very well, remembered how many times it had taken them straight to bed.

"I already told you I can keep up."

He took in a quiet breath, reminding himself that Maggie was a married woman who wanted to work for him. The last thing he needed to be thinking about was how her fiery need for independence had played out between the sheets.

"Yeah, well, maybe I want some kind of proof."

She smiled sweetly, calmly. "In a couple of months, I'm not going to be pregnant anymore. Then you're going to be sorry you lost the chance to hire me."

A laugh escaped. Dear God. This really was his Maggie. Fiery one minute, serene the next. And the common sense, logical Maggie could be every bit as sexy as the impassioned one.

But she was married.

And he was a runaround now.

Having a father who'd abandoned him had made him want commitments, but Maggie leaving him had set him straight on that score. And he'd changed. He wasn't simple Nick Roebuck anymore. The guy who hadn't taken his father's name. The guy who wanted commitments. A wife. Family. Nope. Nick Roebuck was gone. He was now Nick Andreas, playboy.

"Besides, my father needs me."

Shifting in his chair, Nick blew his breath out in a gusty sigh. Who he was didn't matter. Who she was didn't matter. She was off-limits. "I'm sorry about your stepmom."

"Thanks."

"I was out of town or I would have paid my respects."

Her gaze dipped. "I know."

"Was everything—you know—okay?" He nearly bit his tongue for his clumsiness. But what could he say? How could he ask if she and Vicki had mended fences? If they'd ever gotten beyond the fact that Vicki had favored Charlie Jr. over her? If Vicki had ever forgiven Maggie for getting pregnant? If Maggie had ever forgiven Vicki for kicking her out of the house?

"It was fine." She shrugged. "Losing someone is always hard."

Which told him nothing. Not that it was any of his business. He scrambled for something safe to say, but the only thing he could think of was, "Yeah. My father died last January. I know how hard these things can be."

She smiled and her eyes brightened. "Oh, so you met your father? You had a relationship?"

"Yes and no." He tapped his fingers on the edge of his desk, tamping down the sudden, unexpected urge to tell her everything. They weren't friends anymore. She might act like the girl he'd known and loved, but she wasn't. And he wasn't the lovesick boy she'd married.

Still, he couldn't ignore her question. "I met my father but we didn't really have a relationship. Unless you call having dinner every other year a relationship."

"That's too bad." Genuine regret colored her voice. "So how's your mom?"

He chuckled. "She's just like a little general at the day-care. Loves the kids, but keeps them in line."

Maggie's laugh was quick and easy. "God I've missed her."

"We missed you." The words slipped out and he knew why. He was getting comfortable with her. And that was wrong. If they were going to work together, he had to draw lines. Be professional.

She looked away. "No point in staying once I'd lost the baby."

Hearing her say that now hurt almost as much as it had the day she'd left. "Right."

"Before I got pregnant, we both had plans."

"Is that what you were thinking about while I was talking to my father's attorney?" For years he'd wondered. What kind of coincidence could it have been that the dad who'd ignored him his entire life suddenly wanted to give him a trust fund? Had it been a gift from fate to Maggie, or a curse of fate for him?

She caught his gaze. "Yes."

When his heart squeezed, he swore at himself inwardly for asking the stupid question. He'd already reasoned all this out in his head. Gotten beyond it. There was no point going over it again. Certainly no point rehashing it with her. Fifteen years had passed and he loved the life he'd built without her.

If they were going to work together, the past would have to be forgotten. His only goal should be to make sure she really did have the education and experience to do the job.

"So you have a business degree?"

"Yes." She shifted on the chair. Her shoulders went

back. Her expression became businesslike. "But I'm not looking down on this job. I think there are a lot of ways I can help you."

"What did you do at your last job?"

"I was an analyst for a firm that put venture capitalist groups together with struggling businesses looking for investors or a buyer."

"Do you know much about manufacturing?"

She laughed. "Most of the businesses looking for investors or buyout are manufacturing companies."

He tapped his pen on the desk. He needed somebody and, as Julie said, Maggie was qualified. Now he and his ex-wife would be spending ten hours a day, six days a week together.

He looked over at her just as she looked at him and the years between them melted away. Her eyes weren't as wary as they had been when she'd walked in the door. Her smile was genuine.

Doubt rumbled through his soul. In the sea of women that he'd dated since he'd hit puberty, she was the only one he'd loved. It had taken almost five years to really get beyond her leaving; years before he stopped hoping every ring of the phone was her calling; years before he stopped looking for her in crowds. One five-minute conversation had already brought an avalanche of memories. This was not going to be easy.

Suddenly the door opened and Julie walked in. "Human Resources called. Before Maggie can actually begin working, she's got to spend the afternoon with them, filling out papers. You won't get to work together until tomorrow."

Maggie said, "Oh."

Nick said, "I hadn't planned on starting on the bid until tomorrow anyway."

Julie motioned for Maggie to follow her and she rose and walked out the door.

He dropped his head to his hands. After weeks of running the multibillion-dollar shipping conglomerate owned by his family, he needed this day out of the office to relax before he jumped into the intense work of the bid.

But the hammock was out. Stirred as his memories were, he'd never sleep. His best bet would be to take a long drive down the coast.

When he was sure Maggie and Julie were halfway to the Human Resources office, he rose from his desk, grabbed his keys and cell phone and headed out.

Five hours later, Maggie Forsythe walked out into the scorching June day and took a quiet, measured breath to calm herself. She'd been so confident when she'd applied for the job as Nick Andreas's assistant. Fifteen years had passed. Plus, her ex-husband, Josh, had done a number on her. The absolute last thing she wanted in this world was to get involved with another man. Yet, when she'd looked at Nick her heart had stopped. Her breathing had stalled. It was as if she was eighteen again and he was hers.

She blew out a frustrated sigh and reminded herself that one person could not possess another. Nick had never really been hers. Just as Josh had never really been hers. Oh, her ex had made the commitment with vows before a clergyman, but he'd cheated on her. And when she'd confronted him, he'd simply left, saying he liked the other woman better.

The sting of the pain of the loss of her marriage rose up in her hot and fresh. She pressed her key into the ignition of her car. She should be immune to men. Forever. But spending a mere five minutes with Nick had caused her brain to fill with memories of happier times. In the fifteen years that had passed, she'd forgotten how much she'd loved him. How gorgeous he was with his curly black hair and nearly black eyes. How commanding.

Calling herself every kind of fool, she pulled her gear-shift into Drive. It didn't matter how attracted she was to Nick Andreas. If she couldn't keep a forty-year-old bald-ing lawyer, she certainly didn't have to worry that she'd somehow attract a thirty-three-year-old gorgeous Greek god. Especially since she'd dumped Nick. For all the right reasons, but she'd still dumped him. Broken his heart. There was no way his pride could get beyond that.

She reached her dad's farm and climbed the front porch steps. After a few seconds of searching, she found her dad in the kitchen.

"How'd it go?" His wet hair had been slicked back as if he'd just come from the shower. His plaid shirt and jeans appeared to be clean. The fact that he'd come in from the fields and showered was a good sign. But there were still shadows in his eyes. Just because he'd had a good day today, it didn't mean he would have a good day tomorrow. That's why she had to stay. His good days might be good, but his bad days were awful.

She smiled. "I got the job."

Surprise flickered across her dad's weathered face. "Well, of course you did. You and Nick have always been friends. There's no reason to believe you wouldn't be friends now."

She turned away. Her dad had always believed that she and Nick had only married because she'd gotten pregnant and when she'd lost the baby there was no reason to be married anymore. He didn't know—no one knew—that the day she'd left Nick, she'd overheard his father's lawyer offer him a five-million-dollar trust fund, as long as he ended their marriage, and overheard Nick refuse.

Emotionally overwrought over losing their baby, she'd made a decision she'd known would hurt him. At the time, she'd believed it for the best, and she actually still believed that. Nick had become the man he never could have been if she'd selfishly let him throw away his trust fund by staying married to her. So she'd packed her bag and gone.

Grabbing an apple from the bowl on the table, she pushed all that out of her mind. It was ancient history. Of no consequence and certainly not something she'd tell a man who'd just lost his wife.

"You should see his office. Everything's sleek, sophisticated, wonderful."

"That's the rumor." Her dad ambled to the refrigerator and pulled out fresh vegetables for a salad. "He's got more money than the rest of the people in town combined."

Pride swelled within her. He'd become as successful as she'd known he could be. Her only real regret was that she'd had to lead Nick to believe she hadn't ever loved him, only married him for their baby. Otherwise, he wouldn't have let her leave. She'd never had a doubt she'd done the right thing, but she also knew her choice meant he'd never again love her.

But she didn't want him to love her. Thanks to her ex, she knew the truth about love. Most of the time it wasn't love at all; it was lust. And even if it was real love, real love died. And when real love died, people were left alone.

Except she wasn't really alone. Her father and new baby needed her. She had a job. A real second chance at a life in the small town she'd loved.

It was smarter to appreciate those things, than to pine for what couldn't be.

CHAPTER TWO

NICK's cell phone rang just as he pulled his Porsche into the garage beneath his beach house. Though it was only a little after five, he'd taken a two-hour drive, made a stop at a crab shack for a late lunch/early dinner, spent another hour walking on a rough, undeveloped stretch of beach and then made the drive home.

And he still didn't feel any better about hiring Maggie.

He turned off the ignition and snatched the phone from the seat beside him. Glancing at the caller ID he saw it was his older brother Darius.

"Hey, old man. What's up?"

"I need you to fly to Saudi Arabia and meet with the prince."

"Me?"

"Since you took my place while Whitney and I were on our honeymoon, you're up-to-date on everything. Plus, you're family. The prince will only meet with family and I can't go right now. Gino is just getting accustomed to having me and Whitney home again. I can't leave him."

Climbing out of his car, Nick winced. He understood that Gino, their one-year-old half brother in Darius's custody, had missed Darius and Whitney, but he couldn't do anything for Andreas Holdings until he got his own bid done.

"You're going to have to call Cade."

"Cade?"

Nick smiled at the resistance in his older brother's voice.

"He hates me."

"Nah, he just doesn't subscribe to Dad's theory that the eldest should rule the family empire." He rifled through his trouser pocket for his keys and unlocked the door that led him to a short flight of stairs. "Being a pain in the ass is his way of keeping you in line."

"What? Raising our baby brother, being newly married and running a global entity isn't enough?"

Nick laughed and tossed his briefcase onto the counter of the butler's pantry that led to the kitchen. Black granite countertops offset by a shiny metallic backsplash and sleek oak cabinets greeted him.

"No one said deciding to be brothers for real would be easy."

Darius sighed. "Yeah, and I guess it's better than all of us pretending the others don't exist."

Nick grunted in agreement. Their dad had been a run-around. Unfaithful to Darius's mom with both Nick and Cade's moms. Only Darius had been acknowledged and that had made things very sticky when their dad had died. But they'd pushed through it.

"That's why I feel free to call you for help," Darius said, bringing the conversation back to his point.

"I can't get away now. The bid is due for the contract that keeps my company afloat. Plus, I just hired a new assistant."

"So you finally hired someone."

"Human Resources hired her."

Darius laughed perceptively. "You don't like her."

"I do like her. At one time I loved her. She's my ex-wife."

Darius coughed loudly as if choking, then said, "Only an idiot would hire an ex-wife."

"We were married as kids, remember? I was eighteen. She was pregnant. It was a long time ago. We hadn't seen each other since the day she left."

"Still, there's got to be baggage there."

He opened a cabinet, found his whiskey and a glass. "No kidding. But my back's up against the wall and she's qualified. I have to deal with it."

"Do you want my advice?"

"Do I have a choice?"

"If I were you I'd talk about the past with her. Get it out in the open and discuss it, so you don't have to waste time tiptoeing around feelings."

Pouring a glass of Jack Daniel's, Nick scowled. Just what he needed. A wonderful conversation wherein Maggie told him about finding the love of her life, getting married and now having a baby. Yeah. Right.

"Fifteen years have passed. We don't need to rehash what happened."

"It's your call, but if you find yourself doing things like drinking in the afternoon, you'll know you're in trouble."

He stopped the glass of whiskey halfway to his mouth. It was after five…sort of still afternoon but close to evening. Ah, hell. Who was he kidding? He was drinking in the afternoon.

Nick threw back the shot of Jack anyway.

Darius laughed. "You know I'm right."

Nick poured another glass of Jack. "Yes, big brother, I know you're right. But that doesn't mean I have to like it."

The next morning, Maggie was standing at a filing cabinet near the window when she saw a black Porsche pull into the front parking space and Nick climb out.

"He's here."

Julie came to attention. "Okay. Don't worry about a thing. You sort of stay behind me. Let me take the brunt of his mood today."

Maggie smiled at Julie. "You already know he's going to be in a mood?"

"An assistant doesn't work with a boss for ten years without knowing when he's going to come in in a mood."

Maggie laughed.

"He's been out of the office for six weeks. Our bread and butter contract is about to expire and we have to rebid it. I'm assuming he thought about that all last night so today he's going to be cranky."

The door of Julie's office opened and Nick walked inside. Sunglasses hid his dark eyes but that only accented his generous mouth and the scruffy day-old growth of beard he hadn't shaved. Dressed in jeans and a T-shirt with sleeves that cupped his rounded biceps—hinting to the muscled chest beneath it—he was as built as an adult as he had been as a young man.

He took off his sunglasses and his dark eyes narrowed as he looked at her. His gaze traveled from her head to the toes of her pumps. Heat suffused her. Especially when she realized he was probably looking at her because she'd been ogling him.

"You don't have to dress like that."

She cleared her throat. "Excuse me."

He waved his sunglasses at her tidy blue suit, flowered blouse and white pumps. "We're five miles from the beach. Half the staff goes surfing before work. I don't think you'll find another pair of high heels in an eight-mile radius. Wear jeans."

With that he put his sunglasses back on, pivoted and walked into his office.

Maggie turned to Julie who was having difficulty stifling a smile. "I told you he'd be in a mood."

Maggie scowled. "In Pittsburgh some women still wear panty hose to work."

Julie's face froze in an expression of pure horror. "Good God."

Maggie shook her head and laughed. "I've been Northernized."

"Well, let's at least lose the jacket. Honey, it's June. It's hot and this is a casual company. And obviously Nick feels uncomfortable with you dressed too formally." She picked up a steno pad and a stack of files and walked toward Nick's office. "Follow me."

After quickly shrugging out of her jacket, Maggie scrambled to get in step behind Julie.

"Those stacks," Julie said, pointing at six tall stacks of files on the conference table in the corner, "are everything you need to work on the new bid, but that's not the priority."

Nick nodded in acknowledgment as Julie took one of the two seats in front of his desk. Maggie quickly sat on the other.

"These," Julie said, waving her stack of files, "are the things we've ignored for six weeks. Today, they're the priority."

One by one, she handed the files in her lap across the desk to Nick. One by one, he addressed the issue. A few times he dictated emails. Once or twice he kept the file saying he'd dash off the email himself. But he never once took off the sunglasses.

When they got through the stack, Julie rose to leave. Maggie followed suit.

"Not you," Nick said, pointing at Maggie. "You stay."

Julie scurried out of the office and closed the door behind her. Nick opened the top drawer of his desk, grabbed a small bottle of over-the-counter painkillers and popped the lid. He shook some into his mouth.

"Headache?"

Raising the sunglasses, he peered beneath the lenses at her. She swallowed. In all the years they'd known each other, he'd never quite scowled at her like that. Which was good because it reminded her that they were now different people. And maybe she shouldn't be taking liberties by asking him if he had a headache.

He dropped the sunglasses to his eyes again. "Hangover. I had a—"

She held out her hand to stop him. "You don't need to tell me. I'm sorry. I'm not a nosy person. I'm not a pushy person. I don't know why I said that. It was rude."

He turned his chair sideways and leaned back. "If I didn't have a rip-roaring hangover, I'd probably lambaste you about now. It might have been fifteen years since we've seen each other, but we can't pretend we don't know each other. We do." He pulled his sunglasses down his nose and caught her gaze. "Intimately."

The way he said *intimately* caused her breath to shiver into her chest. Memories popped up like flowers in a bountiful garden and her cheeks heated. That was when she realized he'd probably said that on purpose. Trying to get a rise out of her.

"So what are you doing? Pushing us to the point where we'll yell at each other?"

"Maybe."

She gaped at him. "Really? I was being sarcastic."

"Yesterday when I told my brother I'd hired my ex-wife, he suggested we needed to talk everything out. I disagreed, but he's right. If we don't talk some of this out, we'll spend weeks being miserable, tiptoeing around each other." He leaned back in his chair. "I don't like it."

"What? You don't want to be uncomfortable so you're making me uncomfortable?"

"Think of it more like ripping off a bandage." He turned his head to look at her, but with the sunglasses on she couldn't really tell if he was looking at her or not. "You can either pull a bandage off slowly and be in pain the whole time or rip it off and be in excruciating pain, but only for a few seconds. I'll take the few seconds."

"And I don't get a vote?"

"Nope. I'm the boss. My rules. We have a bid due in four weeks. Clock's ticking. We can't afford to be miserable or even slightly uncomfortable."

"So we're going to talk?"

"I thought we'd start off with what you've been doing for the past fifteen years."

"I told you I worked for a firm that put venture capitalist groups together with struggling businesses."

"I mean personally."

Her mouth fell open. The last thing she wanted to do was tell him about her miserable marriage. But she had a feeling there was no way out of this. He was the boss. They did have a past. They couldn't pretend they weren't curious. The best she could hope for was that he had a worse story. "If I talk, you talk."

"That's actually the point."

A man who had a worse story than a miserable divorce wouldn't be so quick to agree. She glanced around at his exquisitely decorated office. "Right. I don't think you need to tell me what you've been doing. Your office sort of speaks for itself."

He grinned. "It does, doesn't it?"

Pride reared up inside her. Her marriage might have been a failure, but she wasn't. "I haven't exactly been unsuccessful. I gave up a great job in Pittsburgh to come home and be with my dad."

When she stopped talking, he made a rolling motion with his hand. "And?"

"And?"

"And what else?"

She scowled. Damn it. She didn't want to do this. Her most recent life details were not happy or even positive. She was going to look like an idiot compared to him. Maybe the best thing to do really would be Nick's bandage technique. Tell him about her life quickly, concisely and get it over with.

"Okay." She sighed heavily. "I went to college, got a job in Pittsburgh, married a lawyer—"

He winced. "Really, Maggie? A lawyer?"

Her chin rose. "Not all lawyers are cutthroat. Josh was a very nice man."

He pulled his sunglasses down again. "Was?"

"We're divorced."

His nearly black eyes searched hers, but he didn't say a word.

Still, she could see the wheels turning in his brain. The honest woman in her knew she couldn't race through the truth or even sugarcoat it.

"You want to ask how two people who created a baby could get divorced."

"Yes and no. I just sort of realized that we should have set some ground rules for this discussion. I suddenly feel like I'm prying. Overstepping boundaries." He rubbed his forehead. "I'm going to kick Darius's butt for this idea."

"It's okay." And it was. If only because it forced her to realize that she was foolish to try to pretend she could hide her bad divorce. This was a small town. People would talk. If she didn't give them the real version, they might just make up something worse. Sometimes it really was best to stick with the truth, the whole truth—

Actually that wasn't a good idea either.

Because the bottom line truth between her and Nick was that she had loved him, but led him to believe she didn't. When she'd left him, he'd asked her if she loved him and she'd avoided the question. She hadn't lied. Simply let him draw the conclusion for himself that she didn't love him.

No wonder he was having trouble dealing with her. She'd broken his heart—hurt him—by making him think everything they'd shared in their two-week marriage had been an act.

But they'd been so young.

And he'd been so broke.

They'd just lost their baby. She'd had no more reason to hold him down—hold him back.

She'd genuinely believed she was doing the right thing.

She glanced around his office again. He'd done very well for himself with the five-million-dollar trust fund his father had given him. She wouldn't apologize for making the choice he'd refused to make for himself.

"No. It's not okay." He tossed the sunglasses to his desk, an indication that the painkillers were probably beginning to work on his headache. "I'm going to call tech support and tell them to set you up so that you can go into the accounting system." He swiveled his chair until he was facing front again and picked up the receiver of his phone. "Julie will give you directions to their office. Once they get you set up, just do whatever Julie tells you to do."

He punched a few numbers into the phone. "This is Nick. I'm sending my new assistant down for passwords and access into the accounting records."

He hung up the phone and she rose.

But she paused. Her heart clenched with the achy pain of realizing that he might trust her with passwords, but personally he was wary of her. He'd given her his heart and soul and she'd rejected them. Actually by misleading him into believing she hadn't loved him, she'd made herself look like an opportunist. Making him think she didn't love him was the same as saying she'd only married him because she'd needed a place to live. That wasn't true, but that was how it appeared to him. And now he was wary of her.

Even if she told him she had loved him that wouldn't fix anything because she'd be admitting she'd deliberately misled him. If she didn't, there would always be an odd void between them.

But she had done what she believed was for the best.

She turned and walked out of his office.

Nick worked cloistered behind his closed door all day, but he couldn't concentrate. The last thing he'd expected to hear was that Maggie was divorced. Not because he'd created the image in his head that she was happily married. But because she was pregnant. When she'd told him she was divorced, his first thought had been what kind of husband—what kind of man—leaves a pregnant wife? And he hadn't been able to contain or hide his anger. So he'd hustled her off to tech support.

But almost immediately after she had gone, he remembered that Maggie had left him. He couldn't rule out the possibility that Maggie had been the one to leave her marriage. But why? Even though she hadn't loved Nick, she'd stayed with him for the sake of their baby. Hell, she'd only married him for their baby. He didn't want to believe she'd leave her husband when she was pregnant. Unless her husband had done something—

Damn it! He had to stop thinking about her! It was stupid. Ridiculous. And he shouldn't care. She was now only his assistant. Nothing more.

When Julie popped her head into his office at five and announced she and Maggie were leaving unless he needed some help that evening, he simply said goodbye. There were tons of things they could have worked on that night. Projects to get the facts and figures together for the new bid, but he hadn't been able to get himself out of the emotional frenzy he'd created. He hadn't organized anything enough to be able to assign any of the tasks.

Darius was right. Working with Maggie was going to be hard. Every little step of her past that he learned had the potential to drag him back in time and destroy the focus he needed to work. He should have kept the conversation going. He should have endured her entire story. Hell, the entire story probably would have reminded him he had no right to feel anything for her. Good or bad. Fifteen years had passed. He shouldn't even be angry with her anymore.

But he was.

Damn it.

He was.

Forty minutes after Julie and Maggie had gone, he stepped out of the building and headed for his Porsche. But he saw a tow truck loading a Chrysler Sebring. The poor sap who owned the car would be walking at least a mile because Nick had located his plant as far out of town as he could. But, in a way, finding a stranded employee was good. Doing a favor for somebody was exactly what he needed to get his mind off Maggie.

He slid inside his Porsche, tossing his briefcase behind him. After putting down the top, he drove over to the stranded driver.

"Hey," he yelled over the low hum of the Porsche's powerful engine. "Can I give you a lift?"

Maggie peered around the tow truck driver. Nick almost groaned. This is what happened when a man hired his ex-wife.

"You wouldn't mind?"

He leaned across the seat and opened the car door. "No. Come on."

Maggie said a few things to the tow truck attendant who gave her his card, then she slid onto the seat beside Nick. He waited the time it took for the driver to get into the tow truck and pull away before he followed him out of the parking lot.

"Wow. Nice car."

Stuck behind the slow tow truck, the Porsche wasn't going fast enough for the noise of the air swirling around them to impede conversation. He'd not only heard her comment, he had to answer it.

"Thanks. It was a present to myself for my thirtieth birthday."

"I hope you thanked yourself."

"Driving the car is thanks enough." He sucked in a breath. Questions bombarded his brain. And so did Darius's advice. He and Maggie would have a terrible time working together if they didn't get comfortable with each other. Fate had intervened and handed him another opportunity to be alone with her. He could either take it—and attempt to help them ease beyond their past and the awkwardness between them—or he could spend the next several weeks unable to focus or concentrate. With a bid due that wasn't an option.

"It looks like you could use a new car yourself."

"I could, but I can't afford anything like this."

"So what can you afford?"

She winced. Because they had picked up speed, she had to shout to be heard above the wind whipping by them. "Whatever I can get a loan for."

Julie had told him that Maggie was broke, but that was before he'd found out she was pregnant and divorced. Now the word *broke* took on an entirely different meaning.

"How does a woman who was married, and probably had a house and a two-income family come out of a divorce with nothing?"

"House was mortgaged. Everything else had been bought on credit or leased. Plus, my ex had run up private credit card bills. So we had to sell the house and use the equity to pay off the balances. Technically I'm not in debt, but I don't have any money, either. I'm sort of at even."

The casual way she said it teased an unexpected laugh out of him.

"Why do you think that's funny?"

"I don't think it's funny." He picked up speed. Air punched through the car now. His voice rose the way Maggie's had. "I think the way you said it is funny. You're awfully damned casual about it. I'd be spitting nails."

She caught his gaze. "I had my nail-spitting days. I really loved my ex and he didn't give two cents about me." She put her head back and for a few seconds soaked in the warm sun and the cool air that floated around her, reminding Nick of how she'd been when they were young.

Spontaneous. Full of life. "But that's over now. I'm not going to brood. My baby will be my family."

Relief rippled through him. If he was reading her correctly, she was perfectly fine. Divorced, pregnant and penniless, but fine. He had no reason to worry about her. And, even more amazing, now that they'd talked a bit, he actually felt comfortable around her. The cascading memories of their childhood had stopped. The fear that she might have been hurt and abandoned subsided. So much had changed in her life that she really did seem like a different person to him.

They wound along the stretch of road into town, then drove down Main Street. Seafood restaurants teemed with tourists eating an early supper. Souvenir shops displayed their wares on sunny sidewalks. Past the tourist district, brightly painted houses with blooming flower beds took them out of town. In what seemed like seconds, they were on the stretch of road to Maggie's dad's farm.

Sunshine poured down on them. The scent of the sea air swelled around them. They didn't speak and Nick's mind wandered back to the days when they'd ridden their bikes along this road. Happier days. When they were two kids who were friends. Real friends. Back before that one magical night when they'd gotten carried away and made love.

Love?

He nearly snorted, but caught himself. What did two eighteen-year-olds know about love? The fact that she'd left him had proven to him love didn't exist. That belief had led to a very comfortable dating life. He didn't make false commitments as his dad had. He didn't promise to be around forever and then scramble away when his current mistress got pregnant. He was honest, fair. No strings. No messy involvement. Just good times.

Which was why he'd loved being in New York the past six weeks. The boredom he'd been experiencing in a small town that didn't offer much in the way of nightlife had melted away. Thanks to Darius, he had access to a Park Avenue penthouse and an estate on Montauk. As soon as his bid was in he intended to take full advantage by flying up every weekend.

They reached the lane for the farm. He downshifted and slowly cruised to the house. As soon as the car stopped, she hopped out.

"Thanks."

He said, "You're welcome," but she was already halfway to the porch.

He frowned. She certainly was eager to get away from him. *She* was the one who had hurt *him*. Yet she was mad? Eager to get away from *him*?

He shook his head, telling himself that in a few short weeks he would be spending weekends in New York where there were plenty of women who would remind him of why he'd moved beyond the love of his life.

He rocketed out of her driveway back to the main road and the huge beach house that seemed oddly empty that night.

CHAPTER THREE

THE next day blurred into a stretch of boredom for Maggie. Nick began reviewing data for the new bid, but only called on Julie and Maggie to pull files and search for reports. Time should have passed unremarkably, except Maggie's father couldn't seem to wrap his mind around the fact that he was supposed to drive her to work and pick her up after. She'd had to trudge into the field to find him that morning, and she spent the day fearing he would forget her. At four-thirty, she called to remind him, but, of course, she got the answering machine.

But when she called again at five, she got really lucky and he picked up the phone. She arrived home at a normal time, made a quick supper of salads and hamburgers then suggested they go to the Ice Cream Shack for a treat.

As eager for a break as Maggie was, Charlie Forsythe started his old rattle-trap truck and they rumbled into town.

"Are you ever going to get a new truck?"

"No need."

"It's going to shut down completely one of these days and we won't even have basic transportation."

Her dad glanced over at her. The wind coming in through the open window tossed his graying auburn hair to the side. His green eyes sparkled. "Sure we will." He grinned. "When your car gets fixed."

She rolled her eyes. "I haven't heard from Jimmy yet. I get the feeling I'm bottom of his list."

"When did you take your car there?"

"Monday."

"You should get a call next Monday, telling you what's wrong. Then it'll probably take a week or two to fix it."

"A week or two?" Maggie groaned.

The noisy truck chugged into the overflowing parking lot of the Ice Cream Shack. Because it wasn't on the main drag, but in the back of town, tourists rarely found it and the place was packed with locals. Wooden picnic tables were set up in a cozy arrangement to the left, giving patrons an area to socialize in as they ate their sundaes and cones. In a grassy field to the right, parents and small children played Wiffle Ball, a game just like baseball except with a lightweight plastic bat and airy plastic ball. In a town filled with fun and games for tourists, it was a quiet, normal, small-town respite.

Maggie filled her lungs with the sea-scented air coming in through the open window and suddenly felt like she was home. There was no place that epitomized their small town more than the Ice Cream Shack. The sounds of kids at play on rich green grass. The sight of parents licking cones with one eye on their children. Teens hanging out, getting to know each other.

Pure, unadulterated joy filled her. She was home. Finally home. Really home. No nagging husband. No bills. Just a dad who needed her and a baby to fulfill her.

A real second chance.

She rolled out of the truck. Though she was only six months pregnant and her tummy was barely round enough to be noticeable, she felt like a whale. Knowing she really shouldn't be eating ice cream and adding unnecessary weight, she had a plan. Before she indulged in a vanilla cone, she'd play ball with the kids.

"Are you coming, Dad?"

"Are you kidding? I worked a twelve-hour day in the field. I don't need more exercise to deserve an ice cream cone."

As her dad made his way to the ordering window, Maggie laughed and headed off for the ball game. The sounds of childish giggles drifted to her, resurrecting her joy. Someday she'd bring her little boy or girl to this ice cream stand for a sweet treat and some fun with kids his or her own age.

Standing at the edge of the grassy field, she shielded her eyes from the sun with one hand as she surveyed the group, hoping to find a parent she knew so she could figure out which team to play for.

She didn't see a parent, but spotted Nick's mom, Becky Roebuck. Standing behind home plate, wearing pink capris and a simple white blouse, with her curly blond hair floating around her shoulders, she looked about forty of her fifty-five years.

A little boy stood beside her, getting ready for his turn at bat. Positioning his hands on the bright red plastic bat, Becky said, "Okay, so when the ball comes toward you, you just swing at it like this."

With her hands on top of the little boy's she demonstrated the swinging motion. He giggled.

"See. Simple as pie."

"Yeah, Timmy. Simple as pie. You can do it."

That booming encouragement came from Nick. Maggie followed the sound of his voice, and there he stood. No shirt, cutoff jeans and flip-flops.

The urge to turn and run competed with the urge to

simply take in every beautiful bronze inch of him. The joy of being home was instantly eclipsed by sheer unadulterated lust. His biceps flexed as he scooped up an imaginary ball, practicing while his mom coached the obvious newbie to the game. His tanned skin gleamed in the sunlight.

Her breath caught and pulse scrambled. Her Pittsburgh friends had warned her that pregnancy would send her sex drive off the charts, but she'd barely noticed that particular side effect until the day she'd seen Nick again. Still, she wasn't giving him credit for making her weak with longing. It was safer to believe it was wayward hormones.

But good excuse aside, she still quivered, and she knew getting involved in the game would be just a tad foolhardy. Like tempting fate by dipping your toe into shark-infested waters. Nick hadn't yet noticed her. She could slip away.

She turned to go just as Becky yelled, "Hey! Maggie! Is that you?"

Embarrassment flooded her at the same time that the sound of Becky's voice resonated through her, reminding her of the happy two weeks she and Nick had lived with his mom. The peaceful breakfasts, lunches and dinners. Fun evenings eating popcorn in front of the TV. As a family. A real family. Not a third wheel as she'd always been in her own home.

She stopped and faced Becky with a smile. "It's me."

"Did you come here to play some Wiffle Ball?"

She instinctively glanced back at Nick. His smile was gone. In its place was the wary expression he wore at the office.

Not giving her a chance to reply, Becky jogged over and enfolded her in a huge, motherly hug before she kissed her cheek. "Of course you came to play!" She pulled away and held Maggie an arm's distance so she could inspect her. "I have missed you!"

Tears filled Maggie's eyes. "I have missed you, too."

"So why didn't you ever visit?"

That was a loaded question. Where would she start? She could fall back on the truth that everybody knew. She and Vicki had never gotten along. Or she could state the obvious. She'd hurt Nick and hadn't wanted to face that, either. Or she could say the convenient. Her husband hated what he called her grubby little North Carolina tourist pit town.

In the end, she said only, "There never seemed to be time. I had a busy job. My husband was always at the beck and call of his clients."

Becky glanced around. "Where is your husband?"

"We're divorced."

That caused sweet Becky's face to fall in sadness. "I'm so sorry."

The freedom she'd felt when she and her dad had first pulled into The Shack wove through her again. Her marriage might have seemed okay, but in the past few days Maggie had come to realize her ex-husband was a spend-aholic narcissist who'd never been particularly affectionate and who had ruled her. The truth was she'd never been what anybody would call happy. The sweet knowledge that she had a chance to start over, in her hometown, as herself, with no one telling her what to do filled her again.

Her lips tugged upward into a smile. "Don't be sorry. The more I'm divorced from him the more I'm coming to see it might not have been such a bad thing."

Becky looped her arm through Maggie's. "Since it brought you back to Ocean Palms, I'm afraid I'm going to have to agree." She nudged Maggie's shoulder. "Now what position do you want to play?"

Considering that Nick had already seen her—so there was no hiding from him—and noticing that the kids were getting antsy, she didn't argue. She glanced at the field and saw most of the important positions were filled by parents with a smattering of little kids in between, probably learning the ropes of the game. "How about shortstop?"

Becky patted her arm. "Perfect. We haven't had a shortstop in decades."

Maggie laughed and walked to her position. Taking a quick look to get the lay of the field, she noticed Nick was only a few yards behind her and waved. "Hey."

What else could she do? He might be her boss, ex-husband, first lover, but this was a small town. They were bound to run into each other.

"Hey."

His deep, gruff voice drifted to her just as a big bruiser of a boy stepped up to the plate, took a swipe at the first pitch and sent the ball flying to Maggie.

She held up her hands. "I've got it!"

But two seconds before the little plastic ball would have slapped into her hands, Nick cut in front of her and snatched it from the air.

"You're out, Timmy," he called, tossing the ball back to the pitcher, a freckle-faced girl who wore her dark hair in pigtails.

Nick turned to flounce away, but Maggie caught his arm. "That was my ball and I had it."

He glanced at her hand holding his magnificent biceps. Myriad emotions passed through his eyes. The anger blew right by her in favor of the little glimmer of attraction that sparkled in the dark depths of his nearly black eyes. She sucked in a breath. That one little glimmer lit a match under her overactive libido again. Her tummy tightened. Her blood sang in her veins. Her muscles melted. A very familiar sizzle arched between them.

She dropped his arm like a hot potato.

Stepping back, she calmed her voice, as she said, "You shouldn't have jumped in front of me."

He snorted and turned to go back to his place in the outfield. "Right."

"Hey!" She nearly grabbed him again to keep him from dismissing her, but she remembered the sizzle and fisted her hands at her sides. "I'm a good player."

"You're stale."

"And this is a pickup Wiffle Ball game, Mr. Macho! Not the World Series." Memories of how her ex had bossed her in the past two years filled her with righteous indignation. If she was here to be free, then she intended to be free. "You don't have to cover for me."

The next three kids hit low ground balls. Two whizzed right by the pitcher and both kids got on base. With two outs and two kids on, the next pitch could result in either the necessary out to end the inning or a run scored.

Maggie wiped sweat off her brow. Though it was after seven, heat still held the tiny town in a vise grip.

Nick called for a time-out and ambled over to her. "Are you okay?"

She looked around. "Yes." Her face scrunched in confusion. "Did you just call time to check on me?"

"You look awful."

She laughed. "Thanks."

"No. I'm serious. You look terrible. Like you're going to faint from heat."

Her gaze involuntarily fell to the sweat glistening on his pecs. She shook her head. "You should talk. You look hotter than I feel."

Too late she realized how that sounded and she clamped her mouth shut.

But everything inside of Nick stilled as he felt himself being slapped back in time. Back to when comments like that could set his blood on fire and make him want to take her right where they stood. It infuriated him that she still had that power, but when he saw her face heat with embarrassment, a thrill of male pride raced through him. Well, well, well. Sweet little I-don't-love-you Maggie wasn't so unaffected after all. If nothing else, she remembered how good they had been in bed.

He laughed and winked at her. "So I guess I've still got it."

She grabbed his shoulders and turned him around, giving him a shove to send him back to the outfield. He scooted off, pretending to be unaffected and not wanting to make a scene or call too much attention to them, but the skin she'd touched tingled. His body had tensed in anticipation. His blood shimmered in his veins.

He rationalized it away. He would always equate Maggie with sex, sex appeal. Because she was the first woman he'd touched, the first woman he'd tasted, no one had ever compared.

But he'd had lots of women since Maggie and intended to take advantage of the new group he'd begun meeting in New York City. He didn't need to flirt with Maggie. Not even out of boredom.

A little girl with a yellow ponytail got up to bat and hit a line drive right to Maggie. As naturally as if she'd been doing it every day for the past fifteen years, she bent and scooped up the ball. Unfortunately Nick was treated to a picture of her perfect butt and long, shapely legs.

He blinked a few times then spun away as she wailed the ball to the first baseman, who caught it effortlessly, getting the third out that retired the side.

Maggie jumped for joy, whooped and hollered, as she high-fived the dark-haired boy manning first base.

Unimaginable joy hit Nick like a freight train. Memories

of their past collided with the knowledge that she was home. Really home. He couldn't stop it. He couldn't fight it. He couldn't rationalize it away. The truth of it took hold and wouldn't let go. Not even when he reminded himself that he didn't like her anymore and had a good plan for his life that included meeting new people, going to clubs, entertaining in a penthouse. Out in the bright sunshine, doing the things they used to do as children, then teens, then lovers, he couldn't stop the memories, the feelings that erupted like a geyser.

Angry with himself, he took his time walking to the bench that served as a dugout. The team of six-, seven-, eight-, nine- and ten-year-olds continued to high-five Maggie as they grabbed their juice boxes and talked smack about how good they were.

Unofficial coach, Bill Taylor, Bobby Taylor's dad, wrapped her in a bear hug that speared Nick with unwanted jealousy and sent his anger with himself into the stratosphere. Calling himself an idiot, he took a juice box from the metal tub his mom provided and sat at the end of the bench.

Maggie scooted over to him. He pretended not to notice by taking a long drink from the child's juice box that seemed to get lost in his adult-size hand. But there was only so long a man could drink. When he pulled the box away, Maggie stood in front of him. Her long legs peeked out from white shorts. Her huge grin charmed him.

"I told you I didn't need help."

Annoyance skittered through him. She didn't seem to have the same problem he did with being together. While he suffered the torment of the sexually aroused damned, she appeared perfectly content to be around him as a friend.

Of course she wasn't the one who'd been in love. She

was the one who'd left. And maybe if he would continually remind himself of that he could get rid of the weird feelings that filled his gut every time he looked at her.

"I didn't really think you needed help."

Her green eyes sparkled and the fire in his belly sent a shower of sparks through him. "Then why bounce in front of me to catch that fly ball?"

This was not working.

He rose from the bench, inched away from her. "I didn't want you to get hurt."

She gaped at him. "Hurt?"

"You're pregnant," he said, stupidly, as if she needed a reminder.

Her face fell. The sparkle in her eyes morphed into a look of confusion. "It's Wiffle Ball. The ball is so light we don't even need mitts." She laughed. "The worst that could happen is that I'd get a sting."

Her laughter raced through him like a potent drug. The desire to flirt with her, to kiss her, just to enjoy her, exploded and sent longing skittering along his nerve endings.

"Right." He turned and walked away. But all his senses were engaged. His brain, too. He'd always loved sparring with Maggie. Tussling. Playing. Now, he didn't even feel he was allowed to talk to her and somehow it made the temptation even stronger.

He almost snorted a laugh, but caught it. Wouldn't he look like a pathetic sap if she realized he still had the hots for her?

He got into his car and headed down the coast, then slapped the steering wheel. This was ridiculous. He couldn't take an eighty-mile drive every time he saw her. Why couldn't he get ahold of himself? He whipped his car around and headed home.

As soon as he turned onto his street, he saw the big black SUV parked in front of his house. Leaning against the driver's-side door was his brother Cade. Wearing his usual Stetson, jeans and boots, he looked like an indolent cowboy, not the billionaire oilman that he was.

As Nick had pulled his car beneath his house, Cade slipped under the garage door and opened his Porsche door for him.

"I thought you were on your way to New York to talk to Darius before you flew to Saudi Arabia."

He slapped Nick on the back. "That's the thing about a private plane. I can stop where I want. And I wanted to kick your behind for telling Darius to send me to Saudi when you were the one he called first."

He motioned for Cade to precede him up the steps into the kitchen. This was exactly what he needed. A good scrap with his brother to work off some of the emotion simmering through him.

"Sorry. I'm busy."

"Like I'm not?"

"You probably are, but I just spent six weeks in New York, babysitting Andreas Holdings while you sat in your comfy chair in your ranch house probably watching reruns of *Lost*."

Cade snorted.

And Nick relaxed. They'd sit on old lawn chairs beneath the deck, watch the ocean, drink some beer.

"Yeah, well at least I didn't hire my ex-wife."

His dying irritation with himself for hiring Maggie burst into flames again. Still, there was no way he'd let Cade see that. He opened the fridge, pulled out two cold ones and tossed one to Cade. "I'll have to thank Darius for being able to keep a secret."

"Hey, when we decided to be brothers for real, we agreed there would be no more secrets."

"Right." When they were talking about Darius and Gino that had been a great idea. When it came to himself, Nick wasn't exactly thrilled with the no secrets policy. He pointed at the French doors that led to the deck. "That way. We'll pull the old lawn chairs out of the garage, stick them in the sand and watch the ocean and the stars."

Cade nodded and led the way. But the second they were comfortably settled with their chairs in the warm summer sand, Cade said, "So what's she like?"

There was just no changing the subject with a persistent half brother. He sighed and decided to be honest. "The same. Pretty. Tall, but sort of delicate."

Cade laughed. "Delicate? What guy in his right mind says delicate? I don't even use the delicate cycle in my washer."

Fresh annoyance rippled through Nick. Once again, she had him thinking of flowers and girlie words. Just like the sap he'd been at eighteen.

"You still have the hots for her or what?"

"Buzz off."

Cade hooted another laugh. "You *do*!"

"Great. Fine. Whatever. I'm still attracted to my ex-wife. Something like that doesn't just go away."

Cade took a slug of beer. "Sure it does. I have two foremen who cross the street rather than walk by their exes." He peered at Nick. "You should just sleep with her."

Nick almost spit out his beer. "You're crazy."

"I'm serious. Get her out of your system."

"Right."

"Okay, think it through. You have some sort of idealized picture of her in your head. Like she was the special love of your life or something."

Nick scowled, but what Cade said made sense. He hadn't thought about love or even commitments in fifteen years, and Maggie comes back and suddenly it was all he could think about.

"Over the years, you've probably forgotten all the bad stuff, all the stuff that makes her human and you only remember the good."

Nick peered over.

"So what you're remembering isn't true."

Sucking in a breath, Nick said, "I can't just sleep with her."

"Why not?"

"Because I'd be using her."

"How do you know she's not feeling the same things you are? Darius said she's divorced. Maybe she got divorced because her husband never measured up to *you* and now she's back, conveniently working for you—"

"And coming to the pickup Wiffle Ball game at the Shack."

Cade squinted his eyes in question.

"My mom runs the daycare. Knows all the kids. So every other night or so she goes to the Ice Cream Shack, gathers the local kids and entertains them with a game of Wiffle Ball so their parents can have a few minutes of peace."

Cade smiled. "And your ex was there?"

Nick nodded.

Cade laughed triumphantly. "I'm saying she's just as curious about you as you are about her." He took a long drink of beer, then said, "Test the water, bro, and you'll see I'm right. She's here to check you out."

The purely male part of Nick ate that up like candy. The male ego she'd battered needed to hear it.

"Chances are you both built the other into something

you're not," Cade continued, looking out at the ocean as if what he was saying was of very little consequence. A simple answer. An easy way to get both him and Maggie back to normal. "You sleep together once. You both realize you're not the wonderful demigods you've built each other into. And you move on."

CHAPTER FOUR

MAGGIE tossed and turned that night, upset because Nick was upset. She hadn't come home to remind him of things. She wouldn't even be working for him if there were other options. But she was working with him and they were both going to have to deal with it.

She woke late Thursday morning and couldn't seem to pull herself together in her usual forty minutes. Then she had to find her dad in the field and wait for him to change his boots so he could drive her to work in his old beat-up truck.

At the entrance to Andreas Manufacturing, she jumped out and raced to the building. When she plowed through the door into the office, Nick was waiting for her, leaning against the edge of Julie's desk. She saw his feet first, tanned toes wrapped in the thick straps of his leather sandals, then the long length of jean-covered legs, then his bright orange T-shirt, then his scowl.

Great. "Sorry, I'm late. I forgot I didn't have a car. Had to find dad in the field—"

He stopped her with a short, terse motion of his hand. "Julie called this morning. One of her friends has been taken ill and she flew to Vegas to help care for her."

A burst of fear raced through her. "She's gone?" *No go-between? No safety net?*

"She said she'd put in her time and was done."

"I don't get a training period?"

His gaze caught hers. "Do you need one?"

"No." She lifted her chin. She was fine with the work. It was the go-between they needed. But it would be a cold, frosty day in hell before she'd admit that to him. "No. I'm okay."

He pushed away from the desk. "Good."

Heading into his office, he turned away from her and she couldn't stop her gaze from skimming down his back and nearly perfect butt.

Good Lord. Would she ever be able to look at him without thinking of those two weeks they were married? Without thinking about making love, discovering sex… discovering each other? How proud she was to be married to him? How happy she'd been?

She shook her head. Being attracted to him was crazy. Not only had fifteen long years passed, but also she was living a second chance. Second chances did not come along every day. She did not intend to screw up by falling for a man who might be attracted to her but wouldn't really "want" her because she'd hurt him. So why she was having these thoughts was beyond her.

At his office door, he suddenly stopped and pivoted to face her. "Well, come on. Stow your gear then bring a pad and pen into my office and we'll get started."

Grateful that she'd brought her eyes away from his butt before he'd turned, Maggie nodded. She tossed her purse and sandwich into her desk drawer, grabbed a pad and pen and followed him.

He pointed at the conference table which was piled high with files and loose papers, including mail and messages. Julie had called them the information he'd need to write the bid, but though Nick had been reviewing information all week, he hadn't touched these stacks. So it appeared this was the day she and Nick jumped in.

"You sit there." He indicated a chair on the right side. "I'll sit here." He grabbed the back of the seat at the head of the table, pulled it out and sat, putting them catty-cornered from each other. Close enough to touch.

She almost groaned. She didn't understand the ridiculous temptation that continually rose up in her when he was around, except to blame it on pregnancy hormones unleashed the night before when she'd seen him shirtless. Actually, that made sense. Now all she had to do was stifle it.

Looking at the stacks, he drew in a deep breath. "Now the question is where to start."

"I'd go with the files. They're thicker. It'll feel like we're getting more work done."

He scowled, but reached for the files. He pulled a green one off the stack, opened it and began reading.

"Okay," he said, tossing the opened file in front of her. "This is our engineer's analysis of the differences between the product specs from five years ago and the current bid."

He rose and retrieved a cylinder of drawings from his desk. He unrolled it on the conference table. "The part we manufacture has been changed significantly."

She raised her gaze to meet his. "Which will change our bid."

He quickly looked away. "While I was gone, I'm guessing the estimating department already put together the materials numbers. They're waiting for us to call for them. So you do that."

She grabbed her notebook and pen and scribbled the instruction. "Who do I call?"

"Talk to John Sprankle. He's lead estimator. He'll have done the work himself since this is our primary bid."

She smiled. "Great."

He looked away again.

Okay. The first glance away she could think was normal. The second not so much. She didn't have to ask why he was uncomfortable around her. They'd had an awkward time at the ice cream stand. He'd left because of her. She could let it go, let him work through it on his own, but as he'd already said this project was too important for them to be tiptoeing around each other. They had to talk about this. At the very least she had to apologize.

She cleared her throat. "Uh...about yesterday."

He glanced over, his expression guarded. "What about yesterday? Did Julie say something needed to be done?"

"No. I just feel bad that you left the game last night."

He looked away. "Don't be. My younger brother Cade was waiting for me at the house when I got there. He wanted to surprise me."

Happiness bubbled up in her. Nick had always hated being alone. It was wonderful to realize he was getting close to his brothers.

"So what happened?"

"What happened when?"

"With your brother, you dolt." She playfully tapped his forearm. A current of electricity raced up her arm and she was transported back in time. This was how it had started the night they'd gone from friends to lovers. A touch that should have been playful had turned electric. They'd looked into each other's eyes and the spark of electricity had become an avalanche of desire.

He'd kissed her and she'd melted.

Wow. Not a good thing to remember when she was already overheated with pregnancy hormones.

"Is your brother here for a week or the weekend or what?"

Ignoring her, he read over the plans. She should have let him work. She should have been glad he wasn't having the memories she was, should have been glad for the reprieve. But her curiosity was like an overeager child jumping up and down inside her. Questions spilled out before she could stop them.

"Is he tall, is he thin, is he grouchy, is he fun?"

He rolled his head to the side to catch her gaze again. "Why? Want an intro?"

Pain speared her. How little did he think of her? "Are you kidding me? I'm just plain curious and I'm curious for you." She tapped his hand again then held back a groan. He was warm. Solid. His skin rough. Masculine. A magnet for her itching fingers.

He glanced down at her fingers, then back up at her face. Their gazes caught and clung. His eyes sparked with the same need that tormented her.

"Why are you here?"

Caught in his magnetic gaze, she could barely think let alone comprehend a question. "Here?"

"At my company. Working for me?"

"I couldn't get a job anywhere else."

"You wanted to know about Cade…well, he thinks that answer is baloney. He thinks you're here because there's still something between us."

The fire in her belly roared to aching life again. If she said yes, would he kiss her?

Stifling another groan, she reminded herself of the pregnancy hormones. Told herself she was too smart to long for a guy whom she'd jilted, a guy who shouldn't want anything to do with her. But she knew both excuses were, as Cade had so aptly said, baloney. She was attracted to

Nick. Always had been attracted to Nick. And working together had been a foolish, foolish decision.

Except neither of them wanted the attraction and if she nipped this in the bud now, she wouldn't lose her second chance.

"There's nothing between us."

"You're sure."

"I'm sure."

"You lie."

She burst off her chair and paced behind it. "Of course, I'm lying! Dear God, Nick! What purpose would it serve for us to be attracted to each other? None." She laid her hands on her stomach. "I have a baby who needs me. He or she needs me strong and smart. Not caught in a relationship that might only be us trying to recreate something that hadn't worked the first time."

Her reminder was like a bucket of cold water in Nick's face. What an idiot Cade had turned him into. He'd gotten him so stirred up that he'd forgotten the most basic fact about their relationship. *She'd* left him.

She hadn't loved him.

Sleeping together wouldn't solve or prove anything. Except that they found each other attractive. He'd never doubted that. In fact, that was what had shown him the way for his current lifestyle. He and Maggie were so good in bed, she left no doubt that people didn't have to be in love to enjoy each other.

But a smart man also didn't sleep with an assistant he needed.

"You're right. I was out of line. Let's just get back to work." He turned to the specs. "I'm going to dictate language to you that I want you to put into the narrative portion of the bid. Do you take shorthand?"

The relief on her face told him he was right. They

might be attracted to each other but she didn't want to experiment…didn't want him. She only wanted this job.

"No. But I can write really, really fast."

"Great."

He dictated slowly and concisely, his mind fully taken by the complex task. But when Maggie left his office, he ran his hands down his face.

Now he had a reason to want to kick both his brothers' butts.

Amazingly, Maggie's dad remembered to pick her up that night. Nick had been so busy that he hadn't even looked at the clock. But when Charlie Forsythe strolled into her office, still wearing his jeans and work shirt, his hat rolled in his hands, Nick glanced at his watch and saw it was a quarter after seven.

Glad to see her dad, especially since he hadn't yet had a chance to pay his respects, he rose from his seat just in time to hear the old man say, "Charlie Jr. called today."

The eagerness in her dad's voice caused Nick to sit back down.

As Maggie gathered her things from her desk, she said, "That's great."

"Yeah. Still the same old, same old with him, though. Busy. Busy. Busy. Work. Work. Work."

Nick frowned. The old man was picking up his daughter after she'd worked a ten-hour day, yet he didn't seem to notice that as he bragged about the son he'd always adored.

"He's busy," Maggie replied cheerfully.

Nick shook his head, closed his eyes, told himself not to get sucked into Maggie's problems. That was how it had started the last time. She'd always been there for him, so when the tide had turned and he'd realized how alone and abandoned she'd felt in her own family, he'd taken her into his.

He couldn't do it again.

Wouldn't do it again.

But despite his fierce denials, the urge to defend her, to care for her, to comfort her, rose up in him like an angry beast.

"Nick." She poked her head into the office and smiled at him. "My dad's here. So unless you need me, I'm going home."

No matter how much he wanted to take care of her, he couldn't. Hell, she'd yelled at him for stepping in front of her to catch a fly ball. There was no way he could run interference with her dad. He resisted the impulse. "Go." He waved her on, letting her know that her leaving was fine.

But after she had left, he raked his fingers through his hair.

Damn it! He shouldn't care, but the reminder of young Maggie, sad Maggie, needy Maggie, broke his heart.

It was ridiculous. She hadn't thought for more than two heartbeats about leaving him, after she'd lost their baby. She'd hurt him.

So why did he care that she might be lonely?

CHAPTER FIVE

NICK barely slept. He woke early Friday morning and took a quick shower, calling himself every kind of fool for being upset for her when she didn't care about him. Deciding that the sooner he got the bid done, the sooner he could go to New York, help Darius and enjoy the nightlife, he raced to work, and there she sat. Looking like a ray of sunshine at her clean desk.

"Good morning!"

He cleared his throat. "Good morning."

"I got in an hour early this morning and cleared up everything I hadn't gotten through last night so we could get started as soon as you arrived."

"That's good."

When she looked crestfallen at his lackluster response, little shards of pain, like glass, pricked his skin, demanding that he be nicer to her. So he reminded himself that as soon as he got this bid done he could go to New York and he smiled broadly.

"That's great. We have a lot of things to do today. So bring your notebook in and we'll get started."

"Okay." She grabbed her pad and pen and followed him into his office.

Nick tossed his keys and cell phone onto his desk, feeling better, stronger than he had all week. Now that he had himself anchored, nothing she said or did could break his good mood.

This was going to work, Maggie thought, happily scampering behind Nick as he walked into his office. Being honest with him the day before must have really worked. For the first time all week, Nick wasn't grouchy. He wasn't moody. They were finally getting their footing in dealing with each other and could now act like a real boss and assistant.

She happily scooted to the conference table when he motioned for her to sit. As he had the day before, he took the seat at the head of the table, catty-cornered from her. He said nothing. She said nothing. He picked up a file and began reading.

When a whole minute had passed with Nick engrossed in the contents of the file, she set her hands on her lap to keep from fidgeting. After another minute, she knit her fingers together. After the third minute, she glanced around the office.

Sitting close enough to read the framed degrees on the wall, she was surprised to see he not only had his masters but he also had a Ph.D.

"Wow."

He glanced up. "What?"

"You have a Ph.D?"

He turned his attention back to the papers. "Why does that surprise you?"

"Because you started a company at eighteen."

"And went to school at night."

"A lotta nights," she said, unable to keep the admiration out of her voice.

"You have to have knowledge to make a company successful."

"Yeah. Otherwise, it would have been a waste of your five-million-dollar investment."

He stopped reading again, glanced over again. "Excuse me?"

Too late she realized her mistake. He'd never told her about the trust fund his father had offered him. She'd overheard him talking with his dad's lawyer about it.

But what difference did it make? Fifteen years had passed. They'd both moved on. She might as well admit she knew where he'd gotten the money to start his business.

"Your trust fund. I overheard the lawyer telling you about it the day we lost the baby."

He set his pen down, caught her gaze. He said nothing, but his expression compelled her to explain.

"I heard you turn it down. I didn't think it was right for you to lose it."

His eyes narrowed, his gaze turned to stone. "Please do not tell me you left because you heard my dad's lawyer tell me that I couldn't collect the trust since I was married."

"You wouldn't have taken the money otherwise."

He shoved his back against the wall and leaped to his feet. "I didn't want the money!"

His face was a picture of disbelieving horror that sent a shot of uncertainty through her. She refused to give in to it. He might not have wanted it, but he and his mom had needed it. "Oh, come on, Nick. You and your mom had spent your entire life scraping to get by. I was supposed to just stand there and let you turn down five million dollars? I couldn't have lived with myself."

He snorted a laugh. "You couldn't have lived with me not getting the money? Well, live with this." He slammed his hands against the edge of the table and leaned toward her. "I didn't take the money."

"What?"

"I didn't take the money. I didn't want it. I wanted to prove to my dad that I could make it without him and I did."

Shock rendered Maggie speechless.

"So, consulting me before making such a huge decision would have been a good thing."

Unable to process what he was telling her, Maggie swallowed the lump in her throat. "You seriously didn't take it?"

"No." He shook his head as if in total disbelief of what she'd done. Then, without another word, he headed for the door of his office and barreled through hers. She heard the door slam then a minute later the roar of his car's engine, but didn't bother getting up.

Too many emotions roiled through her. Too many thoughts competed for attention.

She'd sacrificed their love so he could collect the money due to him—

And he hadn't taken it.

Nick was halfway through town when his cell phone rang. Shaking with fury, he wanted to ignore it but he noticed the caller was his mom.

He picked it up, sucked in a calming breath and said, "Hey, Mom. What's up?"

"The toilet in my office is overflowing!"

"Get a plumber—"

"I called one but he can't come this morning. Oh, my God, Nick! It's going to run over into the new hardwood and warp it—"

For a woman who had turned into a very shrewd business owner once he was able to give her some financial backing, his mother's lack of understanding of simple things usually made him laugh. Right at this very minute, he wasn't in a laughing mood.

Still, that wasn't his mother's fault. "Okay. Calm down. I'm in the car anyway, I'll be right over."

He made an illegal U-turn and headed for the daycare, the whole time telling himself that Maggie's admission meant nothing. Yes, he'd been too angry to stay in the office with her. And, yes, he hoped she'd leave a note on his desk saying she'd resigned. But the knot in his gut and the pain in his chest were ridiculous. Maggie had left him so long ago, and he was such a different person now, that it shouldn't matter why.

But it did.

And when he let his brain tiptoe into forbidden territory, he knew why it did. But he hauled his thoughts out of there. It served no purpose to consider the fact that she might have loved him. Might have always loved him. Might have left him *because* she had loved him.

He tightened his fingers around his steering wheel as he pulled into the driveway of the neat, redbrick building he'd bought for his mom's daycare when he'd gotten his first multimillion-dollar contract. He counted to four hundred as he walked up to the front door, calming himself, telling himself not to think of Maggie—

The door opened before he could grab the knob. His mom caught his arm and yanked him inside, her floor-length accordion skirt swishing with every move.

"Hurry!"

She dragged him down the hall, past the brightly painted rooms filled with toddlers, elementary school kids and preteens, separated for ease of discipline. Energetic music poured from the toddler room. Three-foot-high kids formed a circle in the elementary age room. Computer monitors blinked in the preteen room.

"Relax, Mom. The water's not going to reach the hardwood unless you've got about eighty gallons gushing out. And even if you did, I think by now you probably have towels sopping up the mess."

Stepping into her office, he could see he was right. She had a mountain of towels in front of the office door, protecting her beloved hardwood.

He stepped over the towels into the bathroom. "See? Everything's fine." He leaned down. "I'll just tighten this knob here that turns off your water and we'll call another plumber."

She leaned against the doorjamb, crossed her arms on her chest. "Why? Can't you fix this?"

"Probably. But I can also afford a plumber."

"And you have to get back to work?"

Not able to lie to his mother, he shrugged.

"Ah. Not going back to work. Hmm. Let's see." She ambled over to the open bathroom door, her skirt moving gaily around her. Bracelets jangled merrily on her wrist. "This is your first week back after being away for six weeks, so you need to be there. But you also hired your ex-wife as an assistant so that might be the problem."

"That certainly didn't take long to get around town."

"A good piece of gossip never does." She smiled. "Once Maggie left the Shack last night, Mary Bryant told us you'd hired her."

He carelessly lifted one shoulder, trying to look unaffected. "It's not a big deal. Maggie and I haven't seen each other in fifteen years. Working together won't be a problem. I'm fine."

She laughed. "No, you're not. I saw you leave the Wiffle Ball game the night before last. You played one inning with her then bolted. I'm not stupid. I figured you didn't like being around her."

Boy, he just couldn't keep anything from his mother. "All right, Kreskin. I'm not fine."

"So what happened this morning that you left?"

He rolled his shoulders, loosening the tightness. "She told me she overheard Dad's lawyer the day she lost the baby. She left so we'd get the money."

His mom blinked then she tilted her head. "But you didn't take the money."

"I know."

"Wow."

"Yeah, wow."

They were quiet for a few seconds. Nick stood perfectly still as his mom studied him, his face, his body language. Finally she said, "You're not just angry. You're surprised."

"I didn't know she'd overheard. So, yeah. I'm surprised."

"Oh, Nicky! Are you lying to me or yourself?" She shook her head, sending her curls bouncing. "It's not the surprise of finding out she overheard the lawyer that bothers you. It's the surprise of hearing why she left."

He squeezed his eyes shut in misery. As if it wasn't bad enough he had to face this, he had a perceptive mom who just wouldn't stop until she'd dragged every damned detail out of him. "Look, Mom. I've got to go."

She caught his arm. "We were in trouble, and Maggie had a big heart. You couldn't expect her to sit by and do nothing when she overheard you turn down five million dollars."

Nick's jaw tightened. "I *loved* her."

"And she loved you."

He forked his fingers through his hair. "No kidding."

She framed his face with her hands and caught his gaze. "That's what's really bothering you. That she loved you?"

The truth of that flashed through him like lightning illuminating a stormy night. He'd forced himself to go on after the loss of the one woman he'd ever truly loved by telling himself that only a schmuck pines for a woman who doesn't love him. Now, realizing she had loved him, everything changed. His heart broke again, only this time for an entirely different reason.

Still, he wouldn't tell his mother that. He wouldn't tell anybody that.

"We were a team. She should have consulted me." He stepped over the mountain of towels again, away from his mom and her penetrating glances and on-point observations. "Have Bernice keep calling plumbers until she finds one who can take an emergency call," he instructed, referring to his mom's office manager, as he walked toward the door. "Have the bill sent to me."

"I can pay my own bills now. But that's besides the point. You're hurt. You're furious. And you shouldn't be."

He rounded on her. "Really? I feel like somebody took my whole life, tossed it in the air and it came down in disjointed pieces that don't make sense."

"Oh, this makes perfect sense. Nick, Maggie had just lost a baby. She was grieving and tired and only eighteen years old."

He pressed his fingers to his eyelids. He hated thinking of Maggie being scared, alone, aching from the loss of their child when he should have been there for her. He *would* have been there for her.

"And now you're going to have to deal with it. Fifteen years have passed. You're a success. She's moved on. Life has gone on. You have to deal with it."

* * *

Maggie spent the morning sitting in her office chair, waiting for Nick to return. He didn't.

In the afternoon, she turned on her computer and cruised the various software, stopping to analyze the accounting programs since she knew that's where most of her responsibilities lay. At five, she packed up, hoping her dad remembered to pick her up. He didn't.

So she called, but no one answered the phone. Assuming he was outside, she waited until five-thirty to call again. Again no answer. Six. No answer. Six-thirty, he picked up the phone, apologized and headed out to get her.

She was waiting by the front gate when the shake-rattle-and-roll truck pulled up. It stopped in front of her, she climbed inside and they headed home.

"I'm sorry I forgot you."

She mustered a smile for her dad. "You're busy. I understand."

"It's just that being outside is so much better for me. Inside reminds me too much of Vicki."

Maggie swallowed and tears welled in her eyes. She'd kept her composure all day. All damned day. She'd sat at her desk, pretended nothing was wrong, prayed that though Nick had left angry—furious—he would spend the day thinking things through and realize she'd done what she'd done because she had loved him and it was the right thing. They were too young to be married, too young to be committed to one person or one course of action for the rest of their lives. He had to see she'd done the right thing.

When he hadn't come back or even called, her gut told her he didn't agree. And she'd faced the possibility that he'd be firing her the next day. And the worst part of it was, she knew Nick was right. They shouldn't be working together. She shouldn't have gotten a job with him. She should have sucked it up and stayed in Pittsburgh.

But her dad needed her.

"I know it must be hard to lose the love of your life." She swallowed. Why did saying that hurt? She'd lost Nick so long ago she'd gotten over it. She'd married someone else. She was pregnant with that man's child. Losing Nick was so far in her past it shouldn't hurt.

He sucked in a breath. "Harder than you'd ever believe. We were a team—"

The tears in her eyes spilled over. She and Nick had been a team. Until that one final decision. A decision she'd made on her own because she knew he'd never choose money over her. No matter how much he and his mom struggled.

Her dad glanced at her. "Are you okay?"

"I'm fine. Hot. Tired." She forced a watery smile. "Pregnant. I cry at the drop of a hat now. You know how hormones are."

"Alleluia. I sure do! I remember how funny Vicki was, pregnant with Charlie Jr. She cried at everything." He laughed as the old truck puttered down Main Street. "But I also know it's probably hard having to get a job while you're pregnant. Still, I think it was a real blessing that you got to work with Nick."

"Really?" That popped out before she could stop it. How could this be a blessing? Only five days in his employ and she'd not only been tossed into a sea of confusion, but she'd hurt him.

Again.

"Well, sure, he's a great guy. Everybody loves him." He glanced over again. "I've heard rumors about year-end bonuses large enough to pay off car loans. The money's great. And let's face it. You need money."

She swallowed. She did need money.

"And health care. You won't get on Nick's insurance before this baby's born, but you will have health care. You just need to save enough to pay the bills when this little one comes."

She did indeed.

"So you're lucky."

No. She wasn't really lucky. She was stuck.

CHAPTER SIX

SATURDAY morning when Nick arrived in the office, Maggie was waiting for him. His curly black hair had been blown around during the drive in his convertible. His red eyes told her he probably hadn't slept.

Their gazes caught, clung. A million questions arched between them. Silence stretched.

Finally Nick broke it. "It's Saturday."

"I know. Julie said we work ten hours a day, six days a week when you have a bid due. You have a bid due. So I'm here."

She didn't know why she'd been optimistic, but she'd honestly thought it would please him that she'd not only remembered he worked Saturdays, but that she'd come in.

Instead he looked away. "Is your car fixed?"

Disappointment trembled through her, followed by a wave of fear. If she said yes, would he fire her because she had a way home? Would she have to go searching for a job in the city? Hope somebody would hire a six-month-pregnant woman knowing she'd need a leave of absence in three months?

Her dad was right. It was a blessing Nick had hired her. She had to keep this job.

"My car isn't fixed. I caught my dad before he went out to the field."

He combed his fingers through his tangled hair then turned and headed for his office. "Okay, bring in a notebook and we'll get started."

Relief forced her breath out in a rush. She grabbed her steno pad and a pen and scrambled after him. As he tossed his cell phone and keys on his desk, she slid onto the chair at the conference table where she'd sat the day before. She glanced at the framed degrees and shame rode her blood. Memories of the expression on his face rolled through her brain, made worse by the disbelief in his voice when he'd told her he hadn't taken his dad's money.

The tension in her tummy jumped three notches.

He ambled over, sat at the head of the table. Reaching for the file he'd been reading the day before, he cleared his throat. "These are production reports." He flopped the open file down in front of her. "Every day we print out a report of how much each employee got done in his or her shift."

He grabbed the next red file and the next and the next, opened each and then stacked them on the table in front of her. "I use them to determine our labor costs and to estimate delivery dates for bids like the one we're working on."

"Okay." The reminder of the bid heartened her. With Julie gone and something so important due, he genuinely needed her. Her spirits brightened a little more. If she could help him, she could prove herself as an assistant and their past would become irrelevant.

"I like to review these in hard copy first." He glanced down at a tablet in front of him and crossed something off on the handwritten list on the top page. "So I want you to go through these files and make sure there's a report for every week."

"Why don't I just run the numbers?"

He didn't look at her, just sarcastically said, "You want to figure the labor costs and the delivery dates?"

She shrugged. "Sure. Why not?"

He sighed. "Just check the reports, print out what isn't there."

Panic tightened her chest. How was she going to prove herself if the only work he'd give her was barely even secretarial?

"Are you refusing to let me run the numbers because I'm a woman? Or because you're mad at me?"

"I take care of the numbers."

"Can't handle a little competition?"

He glared at her. "Competition?"

"Or maybe you just don't like the idea that your assistant can probably do everything you can do."

He set the file down and raised his gaze until it met hers. "Now who's pushing us to have a fight?"

Her heart tripped over itself in her chest. His dark eyes sparked with fury. His mouth was a grim line. The urge to turn and run gripped her, but pure nerve, the kind she hadn't had since she'd left Ocean Palms at eighteen, chased it away.

She was Maggie Forsythe. She was smart. She was strong. And she needed this job.

She leaned forward, invading his personal space. "I'm not pushing us to fight. I just want to do my job."

He leaned forward, too. His eyes a shiny, angry black now. "Sounds to me more like you're taking over."

She edged forward again, daring him to say what was really making him mad, so they could fight it out or just let her do the work she could do. "I always was better at planning than you were."

"You mean you were always pushier."

"If that's what it takes to get things done, then, yes, I'm pushier."

He yanked the rest of the red files from the stack and shoved them at her. "Great. Fine. You run the numbers."

Heart pounding, she rose from her seat, took the files and marched to her desk. She hadn't stood up for herself like that in fifteen years and, by God, it felt good. Not just because she'd won the battle, but because she could do this job. She shouldn't have to fear being fired. Her abilities, not their past, should be all that mattered. If it killed her, she would prove herself to him.

When she was gone, Nick rubbed his hands over his eyes. He was supposed to be furious with her, so why had he just found her bossing him around sexy?

Because it reminded him of *his* Maggie. That was why.

Just like at the ice-cream stand a few nights before, her hair was sleek, straight and youthful. She'd stopped wearing makeup and was wearing jeans and simple T-shirts. She bossed him around. Wanted to get to work. Didn't like foot dragging. Didn't like the tension between them.

Yeah. She definitely was his Maggie.

But his Maggie had left him. Maybe for good reason, but she'd gone. And now, when he was furious, only now learning and dealing with things she'd known for fifteen years, she was casual. Able to work. She'd moved on. He hadn't.

What the hell did it all mean? She'd left because she loved him, not because she hadn't? Was that supposed to make everything better? At least before she'd told him why she'd left, he could justify his lifestyle. He could blame his broken heart for the new man he'd become. The man who wouldn't commit, who refused to fall in love, who thought love was for losers and people like his brother Darius who needed a good woman at his side.

What had made perfect sense now seemed shallow, wrong.

And it shouldn't.

How could she come home, tell him she'd lied to him, and somehow make him feel like the one in the wrong?

Maggie spent the day reviewing the labor reports and the corresponding software, and by three o'clock had generated the numbers Nick needed. He barely thanked her. Instead he rose from his desk, ambled to the conference table and retrieved a yellow file.

"These are the résumés for the individual supervisors and admin personnel involved in the project, along with the education and experience stats on the machinists." He picked up an enormous white binder. "This is our final bid document from five years ago. Read the segment on education and experience and create a document that mimics what we did five years ago using the new information."

She looked at the file, looked at the bid document and looked at him. A real project.

She smiled. "Okay."

"Don't get cocky. There's a lot of work to do. I can't do it all. You're hired to help me and you want to do your job. So do it. Get to work."

Joy bubbled through her. "Okay."

Happier than she'd been in years, she read the appropriate section of the bid document then read all the résumés in the folder. At four-thirty she wasn't anywhere near ready to start putting together the new information, so she called her dad intending to tell him to wait for her call before he came for her. He, of course, didn't answer. At five-thirty she tried again, but again no answer.

At six, she turned her chair so she could watch for him out the window, as she continued to read. But she needn't have bothered. True to form, her dad didn't show up. At seven, he finally picked up the phone.

"Oh, kiddo! I'm sorry."

"Don't worry about it. We seem to be working later than I thought we would."

"Seem to be?"

"We're not actually speaking yet, so I don't know for sure. All I know is that I'm not leaving until he does."

"He's still mad?"

"Either that or he's turned into a real pain in the butt over the years."

She expected her dad to laugh. Instead he sighed. "Years ago you should have told him the stuff you told me last night about his trust fund."

"Uh, Dad. We didn't see each other for fifteen years."

"Then maybe you should have told him the day you left."

She squeezed her eyes shut. Hindsight was always twenty-twenty. But even if it wasn't, she knew in her heart of hearts that Nick never would have let her go if she'd admitted she was only leaving so he could get the trust fund.

Of course, he hadn't taken the trust fund.

She rubbed her temples. Picking apart something that had happened fifteen years ago would not make it any better. "I'll call you when we're done."

"How are you going to know when you're done?"

"When he leaves, I'll call you."

"Okay. Sounds like a plan."

She hung up the phone, proud of herself for staying, but still aching over the awkwardness between her and Nick. For fifteen years she'd considered paving the way for Nick to get his trust fund a noble sacrifice. Now that she knew her leaving had been moot, she had no idea how to handle it in her brain. She could no longer be proud of the decision that had seemed so right, but how could she be angry with herself when she hadn't known Nick wouldn't take the money?

The only thing she could think to do to make it up to him was work. Work hard. Work long. Save him some time and effort.

At eight Nick came out of his office, keys in hand. Surprised to see her, he stopped dead in his tracks.

"What are you still doing here?"

"We work ten-hour days. I'm staying as long as you are."

With any other assistant he would have admired her tenacity. But he just wanted Maggie gone. He knew it wasn't fair. He knew it wasn't right. Especially since she was such a hard worker—a qualified worker. But that was what he felt. Discovering she'd left him so he'd get money that he hadn't taken had turned his very sane, very comfortable life upside down. Every time he looked at her, knowing she'd loved him enough to give up everything she'd wanted, something horrible happened in his heart. It ached. It mourned. It started generating visions about what might have been.

Might have been.

He could have snorted in derision. There was no might have been in life. There was only what was—what had happened. And what had happened was that she'd made a decision they should have made together. She'd betrayed him by not talking to him. She'd made the mistake, but somehow he'd ended up paying for it and he was paying again. With questions that had no relevance. Questions that rattled around in his brain every time he looked at her.

He wanted her gone.

But she wasn't leaving. And he was going to have to learn to deal with this.

With a put-upon sigh, he said, "Gather your things and I'll take you home since we have now officially worked an eleven-hour day."

"That's okay. My dad—"

"Gather your things."

He hadn't meant for his voice to be gruff, but it had been and she quickly grabbed her purse and headed out the door.

They walked to the car in silence. Slid onto the seats in silence. And would have ridden the whole way to her dad's farm in silence, if she hadn't said, "I'm nearly done with the employee stats."

Frustration buffeted him. Did she have to be so good? Couldn't she drop the ball a bit so he could direct some of the anger racing through him to something tangible, something he could deal with?

"It took me about two minutes to find the files for the résumés in the computer. So I didn't have to retype anything, just organize the information." Strands of red hair that sparkled in the setting sun blew across her mouth and she pulled them away. "While I had the original bid, I took the liberty of perusing the whole thing. I saw the amount of work you have to do to get the bid ready and I know you need more help than you're letting on. So you can't fight me at every turn. You need to let go of the past and accept that I can help you."

The cheek! If she thought a little verbal lashing would

get him to forget that she'd betrayed him, she was crazy. He understood what his mom had told him about her miscarriage impacting her thinking that day, but making decisions alone wasn't how they operated. They had been a team and she'd broken their pact. Now she was virtually acting as if nothing had happened, which made him feel crazy, or as if he wasn't keeping up with the program. He didn't want her to be capable and smart. He didn't want her help. He wanted to nurse his anger. He wanted to be mad. He'd mourned her loss for five long years before he could push beyond it. He deserved his anger. He had earned it.

They finally reached her dad's farm. Maggie jumped out and he was just about to pull away when her father stepped out of the house and onto the porch.

Tall and slender, with a thick crop of hair that had darkened over the years from fire-engine red to auburn streaked with gray, Maggie's dad looked vibrant and healthy. He waved. "Hey, Nick!"

He waved back. "Hey, Mr. Forsythe."

"Come on up. Have a beer."

Eager to get away, he called, "No, thanks. It's late. I have to get home."

"Late? It's eight-thirty. Come on! It's been years. Give an old man a few minutes of your time."

It seemed downright wrong to ignore the request of a man who'd just lost his wife. Especially when Nick still hadn't paid his respects. He glanced at Maggie who'd stopped dead in her tracks on the grass. She didn't look happy at her dad's invitation. More like resigned.

Her dad waved again. "Come on! Please."

Nick turned off the Porsche's ignition, got out and headed up toward the house. Birds chirped. Flowers drifted in the breeze. In the distance a horse whinnied.

Maggie led the way to the porch. When she reached

the top step, her dad said, "Get us a few beers, would you, kiddo?"

She smiled slightly and nodded then disappeared behind the screen door. Charlie sat on the swing and Nick ambled over to the porch railing and leaned against it.

"What's it been?"

"Fifteen years."

Charlie shook his head. "Wow. I'm getting old." He shook his head again. "So damned old. Everybody I remember as a kid isn't a kid anymore."

Nick laughed. "We can all say that."

Maggie stepped out of the house and handed a beer to her dad and one to Nick. He refused to meet her gaze, but did say, "Thanks."

She said, "You're welcome," then headed to the door again. "I'm getting out of these jeans."

Her dad laughed. "Good idea."

She pulled open the screen door and walked inside.

"I'm sorry about Vicki."

Charlie nodded. "Thanks." He waited two beats, then peered around until he could look into the house. He quickly faced Nick again. "She married a louse."

In the middle of taking a swig of beer, Nick nearly choked.

"She won't tell you that because she's got a lot of pride. But she spilled the beans the day after her stepmother's funeral. Her ex had an affair with some bimbo at his health club and left Maggie. Then got her pregnant one day when he came back to pick up a few things. Maggie thought they were reuniting. He just wanted one last tumble for old-time's sake. When she told him she was pregnant, he told her he didn't want the baby. He'd pay support, but he never wanted to see it." He took a drink of his beer. "She's been through a lot. I'm grateful that you hired her."

Because he wanted to fire her, shame flooded Nick. The story of her marriage was abysmal, but from the sounds of things Maggie was lucky to get away from that guy. Even better, though, Maggie's dad might brag about Charlie Jr. but he also loved his daughter. And maybe he should focus on that, instead of her lousy marriage.

"You don't have to thank me. She's smart and educated." Wanting to make sure her dad understood Maggie was every bit as good as her half brother, he said, "She's helping me a lot more than Julie ever did." Though it pained him to admit it, he also added, "We're already over half done with the bid. Instead of taking four weeks, it's probably only going to take us three. With her experience, things may even run smoothly when I need to take trips out of town to help my brother."

"You do seem to be gone a lot."

"My dad neglected his companies in the last two years of his life. My brother needs me in New York to help him get the conglomerate back in shape."

Charlie grunted. "Doesn't make a whole lot of sense to me to fix one company by ruining another."

Upstairs in her room Maggie heard her father's comments through her open bedroom window. She fell to the bed, not sure if she should laugh or cry. Not only had her father told her biggest secret to her former husband and new boss, but he was also chastising Nick for being away too much.

"Things are fine."

"Right, I'll bet your dad said the same thing the years he was letting his company go to hell in a ham sandwich."

The sound of Nick's laughter surprised her. He was angry with her, furious. He didn't even want to be around her, but he was stuck with her. Yet he wasn't taking that out on her father.

"Hell in a ham sandwich?"

Her dad grunted. "I never really understood what a handbasket was. Figured a ham sandwich makes more sense, what with the cholesterol and all. The heart attack that gives you will send a person to hell quicker than some damned basket."

Nick laughed again. The sound of it filled her with warm, sweet delight and wrapped her in memories. In some ways it was good that Nick had matured out of the silly boy she'd married and become a serious adult. It helped Maggie keep her perspective. But in others, it seemed a shame that the happy Nick Roebuck was gone. Replaced by Nick Andreas, businessman.

"Anyway." Nick's voice drifted up to her again. "Thanks for the beer. I'd better get home."

"Why don't you stay for supper?"

A pause. "Actually I've got to call my brother, get the rundown on what happened at Andreas Holdings this week."

The swing creaked. "Okay, then. I'll see you on Monday morning when you pick up Maggie for work. Seems to me it's easier for you to pick her up than me to drive her in, since you're going there anyway."

Maggie's face fell in dismay. If she weren't in her bra and panties she probably would have leaned out the window and told Nick her father was a silly old coot who shouldn't be asking for favors. Instead she could only squeeze her eyes shut in misery.

"Unless you're picking her up tomorrow to work on Sunday? I don't like people working on Sundays, you know. Everybody needs a rest. You come by Monday."

Pure mortification turned her face to scarlet.

But Nick said, "Yeah, sure, I'll pick her up."

CHAPTER SEVEN

NICK thought about Maggie's crappy marriage the whole way home. She'd told him about her husband running up debts. Add that to the fact that he'd left a pregnant wife and the guy wouldn't rate high in anybody's book. But the situation hadn't entirely come together in his head until Charlie had told him he'd had an affair. Then the facts snapped in place like puzzle pieces and a picture formed of Maggie struggling, Maggie being at home alone at night, Maggie suffering in silence.

When he got out of his car, he punched the wall of the short stairway leading to his kitchen. He didn't understand the feelings swirling inside of him. He was angry with her. Furious. He shouldn't care that she'd married a cretin who didn't treat her well and left her pregnant and penniless.

But he did care. He didn't want to see Maggie hurt just because she'd hurt him. Only an idiot thought like that and he wasn't an idiot.

He called Darius and got a rundown on the week at Andreas Holdings, but he kept the conversation brief, telling Darius he still had things to read before he went to bed. He didn't want his perceptive brother asking questions he couldn't answer.

Sunday morning he raced to work, knowing he'd have the office to himself and desperately in need of something to think about to get his mind off Maggie. He stayed until eight o'clock that night and grabbed a hot fudge sundae as his dinner on the way home. He fell into bed and slept like the dead.

Monday morning he felt marginally better. Working alone all day Sunday in the silent office, he'd gotten a lot of organizational tasks done. He headed for Andreas Manufacturing ready to tackle some of the more difficult aspects of the bid with Maggie then remembered he was supposed to be picking her up.

As he drove out to the farm, the things Charlie Forsythe had told him flashed to the front of his brain again, and he groaned in misery. As long as he worked with Maggie, he would be trapped in an emotional vortex. He hated what she'd done, but he didn't mean to punish her. Didn't want to see her unhappy. He just wanted away from her. But because of the bid, he was in as much of a bind as she was. She might need the job, but he also needed an assistant. He was simply going to have to figure out a way to deal with her.

When he pulled up to her house, the front door opened and Maggie ran out. She jumped into his car so fast he'd barely rolled to a stop.

For the first time in days, he laughed. "You don't want to risk your dad talking to me again, do you?"

She turned wary green eyes on him. "Would you?"

"He's lonely. He wanted a few minutes of my time. That's all."

Blessedly the conversation stopped there. But remembering the things her father had said, he shifted uncomfortably on his seat. Lord, he wanted to be furious with her. She'd broken his heart because she hadn't consulted him before making a decision that had changed their lives. But he'd become a very rich man, dated lots of women, had a great life—

And she'd been hurt, taken for granted, cast aside.

"I'll be glad when my car is fixed."

All right, already! Fate didn't have to rub his nose in her troubles. He got it. Not only was she a divorced, abandoned pregnant woman, who had to take a job with her angry ex-husband, but her car had broken. Surely to God he could muster enough sympathy to engage in small talk.

He looked over. "I hope you're not angsting about me driving you to work."

"Yes and no. I'm embarrassed that my dad sort of corralled you into this."

"It's fine."

She glanced out the window. "I know. Everything's *fine*. But you and my dad aren't the ones living without transportation. There's more reason to have a car than going back and forth to work. There are times that I'd like to be able to just go. Get out of the house. Get some fresh air."

He thought about his drives along the beach. "I hear that."

"Really?" She peered over at him, her eyes sad, tired. "You live alone. You can have all the privacy you want at your house."

His heart tried to crack open. He wouldn't let it. "Maybe too much privacy. Sometimes it's so quiet I think too much."

She laughed. "That would be the day."

"Oh, come on. It's just you and your dad. How much noise can one fifty-five-year-old guy make?"

"None most of the time." She shrugged then peeked over at him. "He's so preoccupied with keeping himself busy so he doesn't miss Vicki that sometimes we pass like ships in the night."

He forced his attention back to the road, but it was too late. One basic, all-important question had fallen into his brain. How could she want to take care of a dad who'd ignored her once his son was born?

With a sigh, he gave in. If he didn't get the answer, she'd preoccupy his thoughts and he wouldn't get a lick of work done all day.

"So are things okay with your dad?"

"Things?"

"No Charlie Jr. troubles?"

She laughed. "Charlie Jr. troubles?"

Her voice dripped with such incredulity that he grimaced. "I'm remembering the past. You know? How your parents sort of favored Charlie Jr."

"Ah. You're going the whole way back to high school." She smiled. "All that went away when I left for university. Because I worked, I didn't come home for breaks, so they visited me. I sort of had an identity. Was my own person. Had my own place." She shrugged. "I can't explain it. But it was like everything that didn't work at their house, suddenly worked at mine."

He eased back. "So all that stuff from our teen years is gone?"

"Yep." She smiled. "Vicki even made trips up to Pittsburgh without Dad so she could shop at our outlets."

They were quiet for a minute, then she faced him again. "So what about you? You said you and your dad only had dinner once every other year, yet you changed your name from Roebuck to Andreas and even used that name for your company."

Nick grimaced. "Actually it was supposed to be a slap in his face."

"Really? How?"

He glanced at Maggie. The wind tossed her hair. Her

eyes were soft, but serious. Old memories surfaced. Times they'd talked. Confided. He'd never done that with another person. He hadn't even really talked with his brothers about this. And now he couldn't stop himself.

"Think it through. You're Stephone Andreas, known all over the world because you run a multibillion-dollar shipping conglomerate, then suddenly you're not the only Andreas business that comes up when people look you up on Google. There's a tiny company in North Carolina…and guess what? It's run by the son you don't acknowledge."

"Ouch."

He shrugged. "I was young. Angry. I'd thrown my dad's five million dollars back in his face and I wanted him to know I hadn't needed it."

"You regret it."

A statement, not a question.

"Yes." He glanced at her again. "Not refusing the trust, but being such a lunkhead. In my twenties it felt wonderful to be a thorn in his side. But when my company really took root and became well-known in my industry, I started to see what an idiot I was. He might have abandoned my mom and never acknowledged me, but he was trying to make up for that."

"So you forgave him?"

How could he explain to Maggie that he'd become his dad—not completely, but in some ways—so he had no real right to be angry?

He couldn't. So he said simply, "I forgave him."

"I never did hear the story of how you got started without any money."

Eager to be off the topic of his dad, Nick answered without thinking. "I met up with a guy who knew a guy who knew a guy who was not only selling some old equipment, he also had the balance of a contract to finish. So we did the deal on a profit sharing basis—the seller wouldn't get money until the profits were official—and I was in business."

"Smart."

Pride lifted his mood as they reached Andreas Manufacturing. He was smart. He had made it. No one could take that away from him. He pulled his Porsche into his reserved parking space and followed Maggie into the building.

But as they stepped into her office, reality returned. A fierce pang burst in his chest, shoving his pride into another dimension, reminding him she wasn't his friend, only his employee, yet they'd talked. As if she hadn't left him, and there weren't fifteen years between them, he'd told her things he hadn't ever told another person.

Something like fear laced with a warning stole through him. What the hell was he doing? She needed this job. He needed her help. And he also didn't want to hurt her. Nick Roebuck had been the love of her life. Not Nick Andreas. Nick Andreas didn't want to be the love of anybody's life and he had better remember that.

After giving her time to put her lunch bag in a drawer and get settled at her desk, he called her into his office and quickly dictated a few things he needed to be done that morning. Then he went back to work on the bid. He closed the door, kept himself set apart and got back into Nick Andreas mode.

When Maggie returned to her office after eating her sandwich in the employee cafeteria, Nick wasn't back from lunch yet. Bored, she perused the labor files again and was surprised to notice something intriguing.

When Nick suddenly strode past her desk, her head snapped up.

"Hey! I just found the most interesting thing in the labor reports."

He stopped, hesitated then faced her. "What?"

His guarded expression told her that all the goodwill they'd built that morning in the car was now gone. He was back to being angry with her. She had to be okay with that. She had no right to his friendship, only to this job, and she intended to keep it by wearing him down with her abilities.

"This employee Jake Graessle?" She tapped the paper. "Look how the productivity of the person on the machine beside his goes up."

For that, Nick took the few steps over to her desk. He tried to read the paper upside down, but apparently was unable to because he walked behind her desk and stood beside her.

Woodsy aftershave invaded her nostrils. His pure masculine heat wafted to her as he leaned in and read the lines she'd pointed out.

"Interesting."

Forcing herself to ignore his nearness, she said, "If his supervisor is having trouble with another employee's production, he could try an experiment and put him beside Jake. If that employee's stats go up, then we'll know Jake's one of those people who just naturally exerts a sort of positive peer pressure."

With a "Hmm" Nick straightened away. "Call his supervisor in."

She reached for her notepad. "What time do you want to talk to him?"

"You found the data. You have the honor of telling him. And helping him figure out the best way to use it."

Pleasure warmed her blood. "Really?"

"Sure." He didn't look at her as he spoke and his words

were dull, lifeless. "This job can be whatever you want to make it. Julie preferred the secretarial end of things. You're trained differently. I'm not going to stifle you. Go with your gut. Do what needs to be done. Stretch yourself."

Reminding herself that his anger with her was justified, yet he was no longer holding it against her professionally, she let him walk away and called Jake's supervisor to her office. She spent a half hour going over the labor reports and her findings. Liking her recommendations, George Wyman left her office a happy camper. Unfortunately when he had gone, Maggie had nothing to do.

With a deep breath, she pushed herself out of her chair, picked up her steno pad and a pen and walked into Nick's office.

He didn't even glance up. "Yes?"

"I don't have anything to do."

He hesitated, but eventually looked up and pointed at the conference table. "Sit. I'll be right over."

She took her normal seat, but Nick didn't take his. Instead of sitting catty-cornered from her, he sat across from her.

A weird sensation enveloped her. The distance between them felt so wrong, yet what right did she have for things to be anything but strained between them? She shouldn't feel weird. She shouldn't be unhappy. She shouldn't feel anything but gratitude that he kept her in his employ.

He pulled the next file off the stack. It contained hard copies of reports that Julie had generated from the accounting software. He quickly explained that he got some of the reports monthly, some weekly, some daily. Printing all of them and having them on his desk was her duty. Filing hard copies where he could find them when he worked late was also her responsibility.

From there he dictated some correspondence, most of

which he wanted her to send as emails. His voice never wavered from a crisp, efficient monotone. He said nothing nice, nothing personal. In spite of her best efforts to accept that, the temperature in the room went from cool to frigid in the half hour it took him to get through the stack.

Finished, he rose from his seat. "That's all. I think you have enough to keep you busy until quitting time."

She said, "Yes. Thank you," and left his office.

At her desk, she dropped her head into her hands. She might have impressed him enough with her finding about Jake, but he was back to giving her only secretarial tasks again. The good impression she'd made had only been temporary.

She sighed. What did she expect—

Actually she'd expected him to take the damned five million dollars. She'd expected him to be smug about his success, while secretly she could be equally smug about her sacrifice. Instead he'd succeeded without her "help" and was angry that she'd made a decision without him.

She was the loser in all of this.

At five, she didn't even bother letting Nick know she was leaving. He might still be working on the bid, and working ten-hour days, but the work he'd given her that afternoon was his regular assistant day-to-day work. And she was finished. She had nothing else to do. No reason to stay.

She called her dad and left a message on the answering machine to remind him to come and get her before she gathered her things. She had her cell phone. There was no reason to wait twenty feet away from a man so cool icicles were forming on the doorway between them.

She ambled out to the warm, sunny parking lot. That's when she remembered her dad had asked Nick to be her ride to and from work. Even if he listened to the message she'd left on the answering machine, he'd think it was from the week before. She was going to have to go back inside.

She groaned and turned toward the building again but didn't take a step.

Couldn't fate give her a break here? Did she have to embarrass herself by going back to the office and either sitting there with nothing to do or tapping on Nick's door frame begging for work?

She waited a minute. Hoped someone from another department would be leaving and she could ask for a lift. But no one came out of the building. It had taken her long enough to gather her things that everyone from day shift was already gone. The parking lot was silent. Only the hot breeze stirred around her.

She waited another minute or two not sure if she was expecting a fairy godmother to show up with a coach or a coworker to return for something they'd forgotten. But no one appeared.

Straightening her shoulders she headed back inside. It was ridiculously unfair of fate to put her in this disgustingly humiliating position, but there was nothing she could do about it.

She breezed into her office. They were supposed to be working ten-hour days. So she was supposed to stay. And work. Not just sit at her desk waiting for Nick to emerge from his office and grace her with something to keep her occupied.

Angry, she rapped on his door frame. "Hey. I'm sorry, but I don't have anything to do again." She said the words in a rush before she could lose courage. "Could you give me something—anything—to do until you're ready to go?"

"We can go now." He rose from his seat and grabbed

his cell phone and keys from beside a stack of papers on his desk.

Embarrassment flared, fueled by humiliation. If she ever met fate in person, she swore to God she was going to kick its butt.

"You don't have to take me home right this minute. Just give me work to do until you're ready to go."

"I'm ready now." The truth was Nick had been watching her outside his window. He'd seen her stride out to the parking lot as if expecting to see her dad, then turn and look at the door as if finally remembering *he* was her ride. He should have simply left his desk right then and there and taken her home. Instead he'd sat in his office, watching her, because he just wasn't ready to deal with her.

When she'd asked him for work that afternoon, he'd barely been able to sit at the table with her. She smelled good. She looked fantastic. Her soft voice tickled along his spine. It had taken a monumental effort to stay in the same room as they sifted through the files on his conference table. And now he had to drive her home. In his little car, where she'd be six inches away from his fingertips. Somehow or another his hormones had not gotten the message that she was still the enemy. And that made him even angrier with himself.

"I didn't mean for you to drop everything for me—"

Her conciliatory answer turned his anger into disappointment in himself. Wasn't he a better man than this? He could understand not wanting to be friendly with her, but why was he so angry?

"It's fine."

"Thanks."

As he rounded the desk, she turned and, from the side, the protruding stomach that was barely noticeable totally changed her profile. Wounded male pride crackled through him like the sting of a whip. They hadn't just lost each other the day she'd left; they'd lost a baby. They'd lost plans and dreams and hopes…and everything. Had she stayed, there would have been other babies. He'd be a dad now. Not a womanizer. He'd have a houseful of kids and a devoted wife, something to come home to other than silence, something that would have him so grounded he wouldn't long to go back to New York City on the pretense of helping his brother, but actually to enjoy the nightlife.

He'd be a dad.

But she'd made their choices. And he'd made his. Changed who he was. Changed what he wanted. Now he had to live with them.

He motioned for her to precede him out of the office and followed her to his car. The sleek line of her back caught his attention. Just as with their pregnancy, she hadn't gained a lot of weight. The taut muscles of her back curved slightly at her waist then flared into perfectly rounded hips. She'd always worried that she was too thin, too much of a tomboy to be sexy, but he'd loved her exactly the way she was. Her skin felt like velvet, tasted like honey—

He stifled a groan. Really? Was he going to let his hormones rule? Was he going to let himself remember things that might be nothing more than an idealized vision he created because she was his first? Was he that confused or that much of a sap? Fifteen years ago, he might have loved her, might have wanted to be a dad, but after five years of mourning and ten years of being a very happy, very rich bachelor, that part of him was dust. He was who he was. Somebody halfway between his unfaithful dad and superfaithful, supertrusting, eighteen-year-old Nick Roebuck.

He was Nick Andreas. And Nick Andreas wasn't a sappy kid.

She jumped into the passenger side and he slid behind the steering wheel.

"I really appreciate this."

"It's not a big deal."

They were silent as he maneuvered out of the parking lot and through town. This drive, he wouldn't be so foolish as to engage her in conversation. He'd already told her too much about himself. He wouldn't give her false hope that everything between them could be okay and they could be friends. They couldn't.

When they arrived at the farm, she glanced over, smiled and said, "You know, I just really want to say one thing then we can never talk about personal things again."

He didn't reply. Let his silence tell her that if she wanted to speak that was fine. He'd listen. But there was no guarantee he'd answer her.

"I'm proud of you. You really did everything you set out to do."

Another man might have preened under her praise, but the final layer of his emotions peeled off, revealing the real source of his anger. Pain shimmered through him.

He nodded quickly, nothing more than an indication that he'd heard. Then she hopped out and Nick drove out of the dusty driveway.

Far enough away that she couldn't see him, he slapped his steering wheel. Now he knew why he was so angry with her. Why it still hurt so much that she'd left him even though fifteen years had passed.

She hadn't just left so he'd get a trust fund. She'd left because she hadn't believed he'd succeed. At least not without help.

And that was the real bottom line. She hadn't trusted him. She hadn't believed in him.

The one person he'd always thought would stand by him hadn't.

Because she hadn't believed in him.

CHAPTER EIGHT

THAT night, Nick made his typical call to Darius. But when his older brother didn't answer, he left a message asking him to return the call the next morning.

He didn't want to talk to Darius that night. He was too perceptive. He'd hear something in Nick's voice and he'd drag this part of the story out of him, too. Nick was getting just a bit tired of his entire gloomy past being revealed bit by bit for his brothers' entertainment. It wasn't a matter of keeping a secret; it had become an issue of privacy, of pride.

By the time Darius called the next morning, Nick was in control. Now that he understood the real bottom line to his hurt over Maggie leaving, it was easy to keep his anger under wraps. Also easy to put everything into perspective. He wasn't a sap who hadn't gotten over being left by the woman he'd loved. He was a hardworking, ambitious man who'd been blindsided. The woman he'd put his trust in didn't trust him to become the man he'd known he could be and she'd cast him aside.

There was a reason to be angry. But not stay angry forever. He wouldn't get involved with Maggie again. Not even as a friend. But he could work with her. Hell, he needed her. And with his new perspective, he wouldn't have to fight that anymore.

The balance of the week went smoothly. She didn't force them into any more private conversations and he didn't hesitate to give her work. Hard work. The good jobs she wanted. Not only did that free Nick to do the more complicated tasks only he could handle, but also that seemed to please her. Which meant there were no more questions, no more awkward conversations. Even Saturday flew by without a hitch. They were a happy assistant and a busy boss and life returned to normal.

On Sunday morning, when Darius called and said Andreas Holdings needed him in New York bright and early Monday morning, he didn't hesitate to call Maggie at home. With everything sorted out in his head, she was nothing but an assistant. The work for the bid was ahead of schedule. He could afford a day or two out of the office.

Her dad answered. "Hey, Nick!"

"Hey, Charlie. I have to be in New York first thing in the morning so my brother Cade's sending a plane for me this afternoon. I thought I'd come over and give Maggie instructions for what I need her to do in the two days I'll be gone."

"Well, sure. Come on over. I'll save some lunch."

"Don't save lunch. I'll have about two minutes to talk to her before I have to get myself to the airport."

He hung up the phone and, with a legal pad on his bed, he made a list of things for Maggie to do as he hastily packed.

Flying down the driveway to her dad's farm, he raised a layer of dust that barely had time to disburse before he jumped out of his Porsche.

Instruction sheet in hand, he headed for the front porch steps, but the sound of someone jumping off the diving board of the pool in back of the house caught his attention. He remembered swimming in that pool with Maggie when

they were about six, after her mom had died but before
Vicki came into their lives. Charlie always acted as life-
guard and at least once did a belly flop, trying to dive. Now
that he felt better about the whole situation with Maggie,
he could spare two minutes to tease lonely Charlie about
his dive.

With a happy snicker, he snuck around the side of the
house and stopped dead.

Rather than see Charlie, Nick watched Maggie pull
herself out of the pool. Water ran from her long red hair,
down her arms and legs, and made rivulets down her chest
to her breasts. The top of the bright blue bathing suit she
wore fluffed out around her middle, effectively hiding her
pregnancy. The bottom was cut high enough that every
inch of her long, smooth legs was exposed.

His breath shuddered in and out of his lungs. Good
God.

He hadn't forgotten how beautiful she was. How sexy.
But he had forgotten that nobody did a bathing suit justice
the way Maggie did.

She turned in his direction and surprise registered on
her face when she saw him. She rubbed a towel across
her head to absorb the excess water. "Nick? What are you
doing here?"

As she spoke, she took in his black suit, white shirt and
striped tie. When her gaze drifted down to his Italian loaf-
ers, then roamed to the puddles on the blue and white tiles
around the pool, she winced. "I'll come over to you."

"No. It's fine," he said, sidestepping the little bits of
water. "I called your dad to let you know I was coming."

She grimaced. "He must have forgotten to tell me."

His gaze involuntarily fell to her long legs again but
he immediately jerked his eyes up to her face. "He must

have. I need to talk to you about some things for work tomorrow."

Dropping the towel to a nearby chaise lounge, then stretching out on top of it, she said, "Have a seat."

She pointed to the chaise beside hers, and, not sure what else to do, he walked over. Not wanting to wreck his suit or look like an idiot sprawling on a chaise dressed the way he was, he sat sideways, only to realize that put him only about a foot and a half away from her long, lean body.

She blew her breath out and closed her eyes as if enjoying the sun as she got comfortable.

Glad her eyes were shut, he ran his finger beneath his collar, stretching it away a bit so he could breathe. "I... um... My brother Darius called last night. I'm needed in New York."

She opened her eyes. Peered at him. "But you have a bid due."

"I know, but we got a lot of work done last week. We're ahead of schedule. Plus, you've got a really good handle on what we're doing. So I made a list of things that need to be done." He waved the paper at her. "At the bottom is my cell phone number, along with Julie's number in case you have any questions or can't find anything."

She took the paper from him, scanned it then smiled up at him. "Okay."

The hot Southern sun had turned her normally pale skin a soft brown. Her green eyes sparkled. Her full lips curved smoothly, naturally upward. And all he could think about was how he used to be able to kiss those lips. Run his fingers through her smooth, silky hair. Touch all that soft, soft skin.

Reminding himself she hadn't trusted him, hadn't believed in him, and she was nothing but his assistant—an assistant who really could handle things while he was gone—he cleared his throat. "You're sure? No questions?"

She nodded. "I'm fine." She waved the paper again. "And if I'm not, I can call you."

"Or Julie," he hastily reminded. "She's back from Vegas. If there's anything you need that you can't find, she's the one to call because she'd be the one who filed it."

"Great."

Rising, he inwardly cursed himself for sounding like an idiot. "Great."

Unfortunately she also rose, putting them toe-to-toe.

Heat and need roared through him. He didn't want it. He'd thought he'd dealt with it. From Wednesday through Saturday they'd worked together like a well-oiled machine, any thought of their attraction seemingly forgotten. But here it was. Heating his blood, scrambling his pulse, shifting his breathing.

In the past fifteen years, he'd had girlfriends and lovers. Plenty of them. But no one had ever compared to Maggie. He'd always believed that was because she was his first. His first love. His first lover. His first everything. But the desire currently stealing his breath was different, stronger—

Ack! Why the hell was he thinking like this? Sure, she was gorgeous, and, yes, he was attracted, but she wasn't somehow superior to every other woman on the planet. And they seriously needed to move on.

Hell, twenty minutes ago, he'd been absolutely positive he *had* moved on.

He pointed stupidly toward his car. "I'll just get going then."

"Okay, great."

Unfortunately she was directly in front of him. If he

stepped back, he'd trip over the chaise. Step forward, he'd bring them flush against each other.

The thought brought a vision of her soft breasts meeting his chest, their thighs brushing, their lips meeting and suddenly he realized what was going on. These feelings racing through him weren't about Maggie, but about sex. And why not? She was gorgeous. She was sleek. She was his first. So of course he had a special attraction to her. But it wasn't about feelings. It was about a fantasy. Nothing more.

He stepped sideways.

"I'll be back Tuesday afternoon or Wednesday morning. Not sure which."

"Okay."

He headed for his Porsche.

"And Nick?"

He turned. "Yeah?"

"Thanks."

"For?"

She waved the paper at him. "For having faith in me. I know all this has been hard for you, but I need this chance."

He cleared his throat as unwanted emotion clogged there. Every time he had the situation between them narrowed down to just sex, she reminded him that it had never been just about sex between them. Even if she hadn't loved him, they'd been friends. Best friends. Friends who took care of each other.

But in the end that had actually backfired. She'd taken care of him for so long that when a chance to let him stand on his own two feet had arisen, she hadn't trusted him.

He said, "You're welcome," and walked away.

When he was gone, Maggie snatched her towel off the chaise with a curse and went into the house. In eleven years of working in offices she'd never seen anybody who looked as good in a suit as Nick did. Nothing could add to his dark, brooding handsomeness, but the suit reminded her—and the world—that he was somebody. Somebody important. Somebody to be respected.

And she'd just behaved like a fool. Nerves had had her sitting on the chaise lounge and offering him the seat beside her. If she'd stopped there, she could have almost felt okay about it. But, no. She'd stretched out. Nervously closed her eyes. Then stood up too quickly when he'd tried to leave.

But that was because he hadn't been able to take his eyes off her.

That was the part that made her so nervous she'd acted like a damned fool. The part that made her want to shiver. No one but Nick had ever looked at her that way. As if he was starving and she was a feast. She'd forgotten how much she liked the shimmery, shiny look in his eyes when he couldn't stop his gaze from touching every inch of her.

She'd also forgotten the heady surge of power that coursed through her when his eyes simmered. She'd never felt that with any other man, so she'd always believed she'd imagined it. Or maybe that the burst of feminine power that had raced through her was the reaction of a woman being noticed by a man for the first time. Yet, here she was, fifteen years later, feeling it all again. The rush of adrenaline. The shivers of anticipation. The longing for his touch.

She groaned.

She had better get over this soon because from the way Nick raced away, he wasn't having wonderful, positive feelings about being attracted to her. If he was attracted at all. For all she knew he had only been looking at her to check out the differences in her from when they'd been married.

Or maybe the difference two short weeks had made in her tummy. Her stomach was more pronounced now. Though it wasn't the size of a basketball yet, it had grown. The changes might not be noticeable when he was around every day, but seeing her out of the office he might be noticing different things.

That had to be it.

Even if he had been attracted to her, he wouldn't follow through. Time had passed. And he was rich now. Rumor in town was that he dated constantly. While she'd married the first guy she met at university, he'd become a real playboy.

She glanced down at her tummy. What would a playboy want with her?

Nothing.

"So Cade tells me the whole ex-wife thing isn't working out."

Sitting in the backseat of Darius's limo, Nick looked from Darius to Cade, who snickered. "No secrets, remember?"

"I've thought that pact through and I've decided there's a thin line between not having secrets and giving a person his privacy. And we're crossing over into my privacy, so we need to stop talking about Maggie."

"You're just mad because you still like her and you're not sure how to make a move."

Nick gaped at Cade. "I do not still like her. I do not want to make a move. I want an assistant. I want to be able to go to work and be a boss again, not an ex-husband. Not an ex-lover. And I think we're getting there." He deliberately left out the feelings that had rumbled through him at her pool. There was no point to telling anybody about that since he had no intention of pursuing it. He'd rather tell his brothers about the good week of work they'd put in together. That made them both seem normal, sane.

"She's the best assistant I've ever had. Good enough that I left my bid in her hands without having to worry that my company will go to hell in a ham sandwich—" He paused, remembering that was what Charlie had said, then almost groaned when he realized how much the Forsythes were insinuating themselves into his formerly comfortable life. "I like being able to come up here to work without worrying about Andreas Manufacturing."

Darius's long black limo pulled up the circular driveway in front of the family's Montauk estate. As eldest, he had inherited it and the chairmanship of the company, as well as their half brother Gino, but the house was so big there was plenty of room for all of them. Cade and Nick never stayed anywhere else when they came to New York.

"So, it's working out well," Darius said as he climbed out after the driver opened the door. "Not poorly, as Cade had said."

"Cade wasn't off the mark. The day he visited things were bad, but the tide has turned. She's amazing. Perfect." There. He'd said it. Now his brothers could stop riding him.

Darius headed for the front door. "I'm hoping this means we can start talking about making your work for Andreas Holdings official. Get you a title, an office, responsibilities you can take off my plate."

Not waiting for a reply, Darius walked into the house and Cade caught Nick's arm, stopping him before he could follow Darius into the mansion.

"Okay. Here's the deal. Darius won't tell you this flat-out, but he really needs you here full-time. The chairmanship's enough for him. Add CEO of Andreas Shipping to that and he's working twenty-four seven. He thinks you only want to work part-time, so that's all he's offering, but he needs you here full-time and I think you should step up."

"Step up?"

"Sell your beach house and bring your butt to New York permanently."

"Permanently?" Something like terror gripped his heart. "Sell my beach house?"

"Or keep it for weekends. You're probably going to have to fly down once a month to check on your ex anyway after you put her in charge—"

Nick's head was spinning. "Put Maggie in charge?"

"Sure. I'm not saying you give up your job as CEO. I'm just saying that with fax machines and email, you don't need to be in North Carolina to run your company. You give your ex a title like general manager and let her run the day-to-day stuff and instruct her to send the really important things to you by fax or email."

Nick's head spun even more. First, it had never been his plan to move to New York permanently. Or to sell his house. Second, he couldn't see passing off that much responsibility to a pregnant woman—

"I can't pass everything off to her. She's pregnant."

"So? She's already working. You're just giving her the good office. Your comfy chair. The nice sofa. Hell, put a TV in there and she'd practically have an apartment."

"And what happens to the company while she's out on maternity leave?"

"You run it. You take a leave of absence from Andreas Holdings and I'll fill in for you here."

"Or we could just split the extra work at Andreas Holdings as we have been."

"That's not working out for me. I can shift my schedule

to accommodate a few months while your ex has her baby, but being away one week a month as I have been is wrecking my system. And I can't hire somebody to replace me. I run a ranch and an oil conglomerate. I'd need to find at least two people. Maybe four. You own one company. One person can replace you. You yourself just admitted you left your prime bid in the hands of your ex-wife. You trust her."

Nick rubbed his hand across the back of his neck. Not only had he made this mess by bragging about Maggie, but also he suddenly realized he did trust her with his company. Really trust her. What the hell had happened in the past week?

When Nick only stared at his brother, Cade sighed. "Come on. You love clubbing. You like being out and about. Plus, you love being around Gino. Why not do us all a solid and just make the move?"

Not anywhere near able to wrap his mind around Cade's idea, and absolutely, positively not wanting to argue with his younger brother about something that wasn't any of his business, Nick said, "I'll think about it."

"Think fast." Cade angled his chin to point into the foyer, nudging Nick to look at the happy scene just beyond the front door. Pretty blond-haired, blue-eyed Whitney kissed Darius before she handed one-year-old Gino to him. The little boy wrapped his chubby arms around Darius's neck and hugged him.

"We can't put all the pressure of Andreas Holdings on him anymore. He's got more responsibilities than making us money."

When Nick returned late Tuesday afternoon, Julie was sitting at Maggie's desk. His heart sank before he could stop it. Fear caused his pulse to race. Maggie had gone? She'd quit?

After two days of torment while he considered Cade's plan of leaving his business in Maggie's hands, it just didn't seem right that she'd simply quit. He was literally considering giving her the job of a lifetime. How could she leave? Why would she leave?

The answer to that popped into his head without hesitation. He'd been a crappy boss. A crabby boss. She'd been nothing but eager to please and he'd sniped at her. But they'd gotten along and worked together so well the week before—

Of course, he'd also ogled her by her dad's pool. They couldn't stand within two feet of each other without generating enough electricity to power a small city. And she was pregnant. Broke. Maybe juggling it all was getting to be too much for her? God knew he was having trouble keeping up.

He started to ask, "Where's Maggie?" but before the question was fully formed, Maggie came running into the office. "I saw Nick's car—"

She stopped, caught his gaze.

In his mind's eye, Nick envisioned her pulling herself out of the swimming pool, dripping with water, stretching out on the chaise. The feelings he'd had standing toe-to-toe with her slammed through him. His breathing stuttered. His pulse sped up. All his nerve endings went on red alert.

Oh, yeah. He could absolutely understand why she'd be tired of dealing with this—

Except she hadn't quit. She was right here, ready to work. And he was ogling her again.

Maggie took a step back. Her gaze dropped to the floor. "I couldn't find a few things and called Julie."

"That's fine." He had to stop this. She was a capable, dedicated employee, who was clearly uncomfortable with the fact that he was still attracted to her. Unless he wanted to lose her, he had better rein this in and treat her like the good employee she was. "Actually that's great."

Julie peered around Maggie to catch his gaze. "I sort of figure I owed you a week."

Nick didn't argue. "You did."

Bottle of water in hand, Maggie motioned for him to follow her into his office. Files and papers were strewn across the desk. His computer monitor blinked. Without a second's hesitation, she sat on his chair, hit a few keys on the computer and brought up a new document.

She looked so right, so perfect in his office, sitting at his chair that Cade's suggestion of making her general manager suddenly didn't sound so ridiculous. He set his briefcase on the desk.

"This," she said, proudly pointing at the screen, "is your finished bid."

He slowly rounded the desk. *"Finished?"*

"Sure. It was a piece of cake." She glanced back at him worriedly and quickly said, "Not that your system wasn't working, but you were asking departments to update the old forms and then you were matching the info to the new bid package. It was a lot easier to create the new forms in the computer and add our narrative and numbers from scratch. Especially since I had each department handle its own individual section of the bid."

"A lot easier," Julie said from behind him.

He turned. "You were party to this?"

She grinned. "I just monitored. Maggie's the one who gave out assignments, had the staff create the new documents and plug in their own numbers."

He faced Maggie. "So you're responsible."

Her face reddened. "Only if you're pleased."

"I'm flabbergasted." He caught her gaze. "But I won't say I'm pleased unless the bid is correct. I'm not going to take your word for it."

"Oh, absolutely," she said, jumping from his chair. "Here, you can start reading now."

Giving him the seat, she edged around him. But the space behind the desk was narrow and with her baby bump she couldn't slide through gaps as easily as she could if not pregnant. As he tried to get to the seat and she tried to maneuver away from the seat, they found themselves face-to-face again. Inches apart.

She looked up.

He looked down.

She couldn't disguise the spark that lit her green eyes or the hitch in her breath. The reaction caught him off guard. She was as attracted to him as he was to her?

He gazed into her eyes again.

She *was*.

Now neither one of them could deny it.

They held each other's gaze a moment too long and something strange passed between them. In some ways they were the Maggie Forsythe and Nick Roebuck who'd grown from friends into lovers. In others they were two totally different people. But the new people they'd become were still attracted. Very attracted. And connected. Which explained why he was so angry about the way her ex-husband had treated her. He'd always felt connected to her, responsible for her. Not just like the guy who was supposed to protect her, but also as if she were the other half of the whole they were supposed to create. In some ways over the past fifteen years, he'd always felt just a little lost without her.

But that was wrong.

Completely wrong.

Only a fool felt lost over a woman who hadn't believed in him. Especially a man in his position where confidence was sometimes the most important weapon in his arsenal.

He quickly shifted to the right as she shifted to the left and scrambled around the desk.

Julie headed for the door. "It's close enough to five that I'm leaving for the day." She turned and faced Nick. "Actually, with the bid done, I can't think of a reason to come back tomorrow. Unless you want me to work the other few days I owe you."

"No. That's fine." He smiled at her. "Thanks for coming in. For helping out. I think your debt's paid."

"You're welcome."

With that she left. Nick glanced over at Maggie. She smiled sheepishly and sat on the chair across from his at the desk.

Tension tightened his muscles. Understanding what was happening between them helped him to dismiss it. But it also resurrected his anger. He refused to feel connected to a woman who hadn't believed in him. What kind of a man even considered being attached to a partner who didn't share his vision of himself, didn't believe he could reach his dreams? She'd long ago left him. Her baby wasn't his. Her troubles weren't his.

Plus, his brother needed him. And he wanted a new life. As Cade had said, he loved clubbing. He loved nightlife. He wanted everything New York had to offer. If Maggie really had finished the bid, she might have proven herself qualified to take over as Andreas Manufacturing's general manager. He could leave and she could become the new day-to-day boss, saving only the really big executive work and decisions for him.

Everybody won.

That is, if she'd really gotten the bid done.

Turning his attention to the computer, he tried to read the pages on the screen, but he couldn't focus. He shifted on the chair. Peeked up to see Maggie eagerly awaiting his verdict. And then heard the door close behind Julie who was leaving them unchaperoned.

All right. So they were alone. They might not have a person between them, but they had a nice solid desk. And he had more reason to stay away from her than a man needed. Not just their pasts, but their futures. He was on the verge of offering her the job of a lifetime. In a way, he'd be satisfying the fury that rose inside him every time he thought about how life had cheated her, even as he tucked her away with a good job and a good income so he'd no longer have to worry about her. He wouldn't jeopardize that by letting their attraction get out of hand.

Everything would be fine.

Attempting to ease the stiffness of his muscles, he rose and shrugged out of his jacket. He hung it in a closet and walked back to his chair, unbuttoning the cuffs of his white shirt.

"You don't happen to have a paper copy of the bid, do you?"

She jumped out of her seat. "Sure."

She ran to her office and returned with a document about the size of a ream of paper. She walked over and handed it to him.

Once again they were toe-to-toe. But at least this time there was a ream of paper between them. When their gazes met, the air tightened. Synapses fired, but he simply reminded himself that he had found a way to take care of her, so he'd no longer have to worry about her. If he gave in to the hormones riding roughshod over his emotions, he'd spoil all that.

"Okay, great. So I'm just going to jump right in and start reviewing."

He headed for the conference table where he'd have room to spread out.

She picked up her notepad and followed him. "I'll sit here so that every time you find a mistake, you can tell me the section and page number and I'll make note. We can email our line items to the department that created the page and get it fixed."

He sank to his chair and peered at her dubiously. He'd actually been trying to get her to leave. He'd seen her car in the parking lot. She had a way home. Instead he'd somehow fixed it so they were reviewing the document together.

"It really worked to have each department write its section of the bid?"

"Supervisors were thrilled for the opportunity."

He snorted a laugh.

"I'm serious. Everybody said you do too much. That you could delegate and have more time for yourself."

He snorted again. Fate seemed to be pushing him out the door of his own company.

As she sat on the chair catty-cornered from his, he read the first few pages of the bid, the easy pages, introduction and narrative that answered basic questions about the company, and had to admit he was impressed. The answers were short, concise. No rambling.

He pointed at the sheet. "Who wrote these?"

"I did."

Well, no wonder they were short and concise. She didn't have the knowledge others in the plant did. Of course, that also meant she hadn't muddied the waters with unnecessary information.

He went back to reading. With her legs crossed, her sandal-covered foot swung a centimeter away from his shin. Awareness caused his toes to curl. This wasn't going to work, either.

He stopped reading. "Did the department heads give you backup documentation for their numbers?"

"Yes!" She popped out of her seat, ran into her office and returned with a stack of files—so many files, and such thick files, that it looked like he'd be in the office until the following morning reviewing all the data.

But that was good. He could use that excuse to send her home, telling her he'd make the notes of any problems he found himself because not only was this going to take a long time, but also he needed privacy and quiet to read.

Yeah. That was it. He'd tell her he needed silence to read the bid.

She set the files on the table in front of him and he rose. "Okay, then. Since I have everything I need to review this, you can go."

"Go? I thought I'd be taking notes on the problems you found?"

They weren't exactly standing toe-to-toe, but they were close. He thought to take a step back but refused to be that fussy. Surely he could stand a foot away from her.

"No. I don't want you here. You helped create this. You're prejudiced. I'm sort of an independent proofreader. So you can go home." He waved his hand. "You've obviously worked hard for the past two days and it's after five. Go. I'll be fine."

She looked up at him with big green eyes filled with fear.

His insides twisted. He hated to see her afraid. Especially since she had nothing to fear. He was considering promoting her. Trying to take care of her.

"You did an excellent job," he said, seeking to reassure her, but she didn't stop staring at him. Her green eyes softened, as she studied his face. And pretty soon he realized she wasn't afraid anymore. She was caught. Staring at him because she was as tormented as he was about them. About this thing between them. The attraction that just wouldn't quit even though they were the worst possible two people to be attracted.

He shouldn't like her. She hadn't trusted him.

She shouldn't like him. He was still angry with her.

But his head lowered.

She tipped her face up and stepped closer.

And their lips met.

Sweet memory poured through him. This was Maggie. Sweet, sweet Maggie.

Placing his hands on each side of her head, he tilted it back, deepening the kiss, drinking from her like a thirsty man took water. Her lips parted slightly in what could have been a moan of pleasure. He didn't notice, didn't care, but took advantage and slid his tongue into her mouth.

That time she did moan. The feminine purr drifted to his ears and filled him. Sensation after sensation bombarded him and each one flash-connected to a memory. The roar of the ocean. The brilliance of the sun. The heat of innocence.

He let himself indulge, enjoy. He let his thoughts go back to the idyllic time he'd thought would last forever. But when his hand drifted from her face to her shoulder and down to the opening of her simple blouse, common sense awoke in him. A kiss was one thing, touching quite another.

He broke away. They drifted apart slowly. Their gazes bumped. The sound of their breathing filled the air.

He didn't know what to say. What to do. He felt alive inside. But was he really? Or had that kiss taken them on a trip down memory lane? Was everything he felt simply a reflection of what he expected to feel from the past?

It had to be. He didn't know the new Maggie well enough to want her like this. Kissing her hadn't tested out their attraction. It had only proved they once had chemistry. It was a mistake that did nothing but screw up an otherwise perfect plan.

"I'm sorry."

She blinked. "Sorry?"

"You know we can't be attracted to each other."

"Because we work together."

He took a step back. He couldn't tell her about his thought to promote her until he checked out the bid and dug a little deeper into her credentials. So he clung to the reasonable excuse she'd just offered and even added to it.

"And because we really don't know each other anymore. And it might not be smart to get to know each other. You need this job and I need you. We have a past we probably wouldn't be able to overcome even if we did grow to like each other. So what do you say we just forget this happened?"

She studied him with sad green eyes, and he felt like a heel, a fool. He'd been the one to initiate the kiss. Then he'd dismissed it as if they'd been equally guilty.

Hoping to ease the sadness, he said, "Okay. The kiss was my mistake. I don't know what got into me but I was wrong. We need each other." He stepped away, rounded the conference table to get to the chair he intended to sit in and pulled it out. "Go home. I want to review this without interruption. We'll talk in the morning."

CHAPTER NINE

WEDNESDAY morning a torrential downpour sent rain cascading in sheets along the Carolina coast. By the time Nick made it to the office, Maggie had already shed her raincoat, put her sandwich in the desk drawer and started her computer.

"You might as well just bring your notebook in," he said as he breezed through her office into his. "I got through only half of the bid, but there are problems. Not big ones, just things that need to be addressed and we'll be doing that this morning."

She grabbed paper and pen and followed him inside. Taking the seat at the conference table, she watched him dump his keys and cell phone on the desk.

Confusion and sadness met and mingled in her middle. He'd kissed her the night before out of curiosity. They had so much chemistry crackling between them that it was difficult sometimes to not wonder about it. She'd expected the kiss. She'd also expected the fire that ignited her blood when their lips had touched. What puzzled her had been the sudden hope that burst inside her.

If only for the span of that kiss, she'd believed in miracles. She'd hoped and even prayed that it hadn't been curiosity that had pushed him to kiss her, but an uncontrollable impulse. She didn't care if that impulse had been spawned by memories. Now that she was home she was very much like the Maggie she'd been in her youth. If he'd loved her then he could love her now—

Except she'd hurt him. And that was why he'd pulled away. He'd never get beyond the fact that she'd left him. He was too strong, too proud, too *Nick* to simply forgive her.

The hope in her heart was ridiculous.

Wrong.

He took his seat. "When I got tired of reviewing the bid last night, I checked your résumé. You've never done anything like this bid before. How did you know what to do to pull this thing together?"

She shrugged. "I've analyzed hundreds of bids. Maybe thousands. If a company isn't winning contracts, nine chances out of ten there's either something wrong with the business itself or there's something wrong with their bid numbers."

Not exactly sure how to behave around him, she smiled tentatively. "Your bid was great. All I did was streamline your process. I can see why you win the contract every five years. Andreas Manufacturing is a fabulous company."

He coughed as if uncomfortable with her praise, reminding her so much of the old Nick that she didn't think through the nudge she gave him. It was purely reflex.

"You've got to know you're good."

Their gazes met. The wariness in his expression sent sadness trembling through her. He clearly regretted kissing her the night before. The flickering light of her hope dimmed a little more.

"I made a list of questions or problems I found last night. I want to speak directly with the department supervisors to get the answers but I'd like you to sit in on the sessions."

Her gaze snapped to his. *He wanted her around?*

"Really?"

He looked away. "This is a list of department heads I'll need to see." Leaning in, he set a paper with a list of names in front of her.

The scent of sea air and man drifted to her. Combined with memories of their kiss, it filled her with longing. Desire rose up as quick and as sharp as it had when his lips met hers the night before.

"Your assignment is to call everybody and set appointments."

To get her mind off wanting Nick, she leaned in to look at the sheet he held and their shoulders bumped.

He automatically pulled away.

The dying flame of her hope struggled to find footing, but it couldn't. He might be attracted to her, but he didn't want to be. And he was a strong, determined man. He could ignore a stupid physical attraction.

But he still had it.

After fifteen years apart, *they* still had it.

"Schedule an hour with each department. Stop at noon, then pick up again at one. That way we'll have spoken with all seven supervisors before the end of the day."

At her desk, she picked up the phone, but as the first extension rang, she peeked into his office. Head bent, he labored over the papers in a file, looking smart, capable, and so handsome. The bittersweet ache returned. Except now that she knew he hadn't accepted the trust fund, the ache made her wonder what might have been. If his father hadn't offered him the five-million-dollar trust fund. If she hadn't overheard him refuse to divorce her to qualify for it. If she hadn't felt so guilty over Nick giving up his legacy for her.

If.

If.

If.

Thinking about ifs was foolish.

But it was difficult not to. They were still attracted after fifteen years. Fifteen years. She could only imagine what their marriage might have been like if they'd stayed together, only imagine what they'd be like if they could set aside their differences and sleep together now—

"Yeah, Maggie? What's up?"

Maggie jumped as Mark Nelson's voice boomed to her through her telephone.

Placing a hand on her galloping heart, she said, "Nick wants to see you in his office." She glanced at her schedule. "He's meeting a department head every hour. Since you're the first person I'm calling, you get your choice of time."

"I'll take the first slot."

"Great," she said, penciling him in. She disconnected the call and her gaze slid into Nick's office again.

Why couldn't she get over him?

Because of the meetings, Nick stayed until eleven o'clock that night. He sent Maggie home at seven, telling her he would be leaving right behind her, though he knew it was a lie.

Cade was right. He was still attracted to her. The pull of her was so strong that soon he wouldn't be able to resist it. Eventually he'd seduce her—and then what? Hurt her? Lose her as an assistant? Lose her as a potential general manager?

He couldn't hurt her or take away the job she needed. He had to be the one who moved on. Darius needed him and as Cade had said, it would be much easier for him to find one CEO or general manager to replace him than it would be for Cade to find the small army it would take to shift control of his oil business and ranch.

Finally home, he sank into a leather chair in the game room and turned the TV to a baseball game before dialing Darius's number.

"Late night."

Relieved to hear Darius's voice, Nick relaxed. "Yes. I hope I didn't wake anybody."

"Gino's the only one asleep. Whitney's on the sofa across from me reading depositions."

"Hey, Nick!" she called, her voice loud enough to come to him through the phone.

"Tell Whitney, I said, hey, too."

Darius laughed. "Nick says hey, too." Then his voice turned serious. "So what's up?"

"Cade is right. I should come to work for Andreas Holdings full-time."

"Wow."

"I've been thinking it over since I was in New York on Monday. But more than that, I came home to find my bid is done. Except for proofing and final checks on the numbers, Maggie pretty much got the thing finished."

"She wrote it herself?"

"She had the staff write it."

Darius chuckled. "Well, I'll be damned."

"I know. Cade thinks she could replace me. At the very least, take over as general manager, leaving the executive stuff to be handled by me through phone, fax and email."

"So what's the problem?"

"She doesn't have any experience for this. She was a glorified analyst at her last job."

"But she did your bid."

"Exactly. She knows theory, but has no actual experience running the plant."

"So train her."

"I don't want to tell her that I'm considering her for a job if it doesn't pan out."

"There are never any guarantees with any employee. You've got to jump in and take a risk."

"I know. But this situation is delicate." He rose from his comfy chair, passed his hand through his hair. "I'm worried that I'm seeing things in her that aren't really there because I want so badly to promote her—to give her a chance."

Darius harrumphed. "That's funny. When you were here, you were telling us you felt nothing for her."

He squeezed his eyes shut. As much as he wanted to confide in his brother, he wouldn't. There were some things a man had to handle on his own.

"She's a penniless pregnant woman. I'd be heartless if I didn't feel something for her."

"Pity?"

The word tightened his gut. Maggie would hate it if she thought he pitied her. "No, more like righteous indignation. She didn't deserve what happened to her after we split. I'd like to see her succeed."

"So bring her up for Gino's birthday. I'll check her out. I can run her through her paces without her even realizing I'm backhandedly interviewing her."

That was true. Darius would be objective where he couldn't.

"That sounds great, except how do I get her there? Say my older brother who's never met you would like you to come to our baby brother's first birthday party?"

"Make an excuse about needing her to take notes at a brothers' meeting. Tell her my assistant can't do it because she works for Andreas Holdings and this is a family thing. It would be a conflict of interest because we'll be discussing our plans for our shares of Andreas Holdings."

It was a great idea. Plus, the thought of attending his one-year-old half brother's first birthday party cheered him. He was at a point in his life when he'd realized he'd never have kids of his own. That was the one drawback of his lifestyle. But with one-year-old Gino in the family, he had no worries about an heir or even someone younger to amuse him from time to time. He could teach the kid how to play basketball, teach him to fish, tease him about girls. In general get out all of his pent-up parenting needs anytime they arose.

He loved having a baby brother.

"Okay. Sounds good. We'll be there."

When Nick arrived at Andreas Manufacturing the next morning, Maggie was walking to the entrance. He hurried out of the Porsche to catch up with her and held the building door open for her.

"Thank you."

"You're welcome."

He followed her inside, making her just a tad paranoid. Should she wait for him? Walk beside him? Make small talk?

She wanted to. God knew the hope that sprang to life inside her every time she saw him. That hope wanted her to believe that if she just gave him time, he'd come around.

And then what? Was she ready for this? Was she over Josh?

In some respects, the answer came quickly. How could she pine for a man who not only didn't want her, but had also refused to acknowledge their child? It wasn't exactly easy, but it had definitely been possible for any love she'd had for Josh to die.

But was she ready to move on?

Her smarter self laughed. At this point it didn't matter if she was ready to move on. Nick might give her ten signs a day that he was attracted to her, but he gave her eleven that he didn't want to be. And today would be no different. He'd hold the door, maybe let his gaze linger a little too long on her face or unwittingly stare into her eyes, but he'd snap out of it. Cloister himself in his office. Not say goodbye when he went to lunch.

Any hope she had was foolish. So it didn't matter if she was ready to move on or not.

They entered her office. She turned and walked to her desk. He continued toward his office. But he stopped, faced her.

"I…um…was talking with my brother Darius last night."

"The older one?"

"Yes. The one who lives in New York and runs Andreas Holdings. He's having a birthday party for our one-year-old brother over the weekend and he'd like you to come."

Her heart stopped. Her breathing stuttered to a halt. His family was inviting her to a party? All the way in New York?

"We've having a brothers' meeting Saturday morning and no one from Andreas Holdings can take notes because there'd be a conflict of interest. Darius suggested I bring you up so you can be our stenographer for the meeting."

The pain of stupidity froze her tongue. When would she learn this man didn't want her?

"I…I…"

He glanced at her tummy. "Oh, God, I'm sorry. I forgot you might not be able to travel."

"I can travel."

"Oh."

She heard the awkward tone of his voice. He didn't understand why she hesitated. She was, after all, *his* assistant. An employee who could take the meeting notes without a conflict of interest.

She straightened her shoulders. She was his assistant. If he wanted her to go to New York, she would go to New York.

"I'd love to go. Thank your brother for inviting me."

"Great." He turned to his office door again. "We'll leave tomorrow morning and be staying at the family estate in Montauk. Pack for the beach."

The beach! That perked her up. She might only live a few miles from the shore herself, but between work and not having a car for the first weeks she was in town, she hadn't even gotten close to it yet. Maybe the weekend would be something like a vacation?

Wearing flip-flops, white capris and a sunny yellow tank top, Maggie met Nick at the small private airstrip a few miles outside of Ocean Palms. Only one airplane sat on the tarmac and Nick stood in front of it. She made her way over, carrying her overnight case.

Approaching the plane, she said, "Wow. So this is how the other half lives."

He took her small bag and handed it to a man dressed in a blue pilot's uniform, then motioned for her to climb the short column of steps. "This is how my brother Cade lives. He's the family multibillionaire. He put this plane at my disposal for the next year."

She stopped, faced Nick. "The next year? That's awfully generous."

He batted a hand. "He has seven planes. He won't even miss this one."

Seven planes? The magnitude of the changes in Nick's family situation never ceased to amaze her. Or to remind her that he was so different now that it had been totally wrong for her to think—even for the fleeting few seconds of one blistering kiss—that they fit together anymore.

She stepped inside an area that looked more like a comfy living room than a seating area for a plane. White leather sofas lined both sides. A shiny wooden bar took up the back.

Amazed, she stopped.

"If you're wondering why the space looks so small," Nick said from behind, "that's because there's an office and a bedroom in the rear."

She spun to face him. "Holy cow."

"I know. Only a guy who never stops working would think a plane ride a waste of time. I'll bet he's never once sat up here and just looked out the window. He probably either works or sleeps. Never wasting a minute."

They sat across from each other, each on one of the long sofalike lounges. They buckled up and fell silent as the plane taxied and took off.

In the air, Nick unbuckled his seat belt and headed for the bar. "Drink?"

She glanced down at her tummy. "I don't think so."

"We have orange juice, apple juice and water. Not just alcohol."

She still shook her head. "It's a long flight. I'd rather not be jumping up and down running for the bathroom."

He shrugged. "Suit yourself."

When he sat again, soft drink in hand, Maggie glanced around. After the quick brush with conversation about the plane, they'd run out of things to say. But she refused to sit silently for over two hours.

"So, you have a baby brother."

Nick surprised her by laughing. "It was the damnedest thing."

"I'll bet."

"Oh, you have no idea. Not only did we not know our dad had another son until Dad's lawyer handed him to Darius at the reading of the will, but also the kid owns an equal share of Andreas Holdings."

Because he chuckled when he said it, Maggie tilted her head in question. "That doesn't bother you?"

"Not really. I don't 'need' the money I get from Andreas Holdings. It doesn't matter to me how many ways it's split." He smiled stupidly, fascinating Maggie. She'd never quite seen that expression. "It doesn't hurt that the kid is adorable."

Ah. That's right. Nick loved kids.

"Of course, he's also pure Andreas. Dark eyes. Dark hair. But he's built like a little truck. Big shoulders and arms. If I wasn't absolutely positive we'll be training him to take over Andreas Holdings when we want to retire, the kid could easily be a football player."

Hearing the pride and love in his voice, Maggie smiled. "He sounds cute."

"You'll get to meet him. It's his party we're going to. Plus, since we're staying at the estate, he'll probably be underfoot." He pointed at her tummy. "Maybe you can persuade Whitney to let you get in some practice."

She smiled again. "Maybe."

It almost hurt to see how happy he was. How in love with the little boy. She thought back to their baby, to how she'd always known Nick would be a great dad, and sadness enveloped her. They lapsed into silence. After a few minutes, he opened his briefcase.

Seeing how he'd been forced to spread papers and file folders around him on his seat, she said, "You should just go back in the office if you want to work."

He peered over. "Are you sure?"

She shrugged. "Yeah. I'm fine. In fact, if you need me, I might only have the notebook I brought for the brothers' meeting, but I could probably still put some of your notes in it."

"With the bid done and in, I'm primarily reviewing things to catch myself up." He rose. "But if I need you I'll call."

"Okay."

Ten minutes later she fell asleep and didn't awaken until Nick jostled her shoulder. "Hey, you have to get up. We're about to land and you have to be in a seat belt."

She opened her eyes and found herself staring into his. Crouched in front of her, he was eye level. His hand on her shoulder was comforting. His dark eyes were warm. The softness of his voice was sweet, soothing.

As if he realized she'd caught him in an unguarded moment, he got to his feet and looked away.

Maggie told herself not to make too much out of the expression she saw on his face. Lots of people looked with love upon sleeping people—

That wasn't true. She was reaching, trying to make something that wasn't innocent seem innocent. She didn't know how long he'd been watching her sleep, but he'd been watching her sleep and it had put a soft expression on his face. And he'd invited her to his family's home. Yes, she had to take notes at a meeting, but they could have hired an outsider for that.

Maybe it was crazy-just-waking-up brain, but she

couldn't stop the feeling that something more was going on here.

Again, they landed at a private airstrip. A long black limo was parked close to where the plane stopped. A beautiful blonde dressed in a black sheath and a wide-brimmed black hat stood beside a tall, dark-haired man, wearing a black suit, holding a baby. All three of them wore black sunglasses. That made her laugh. Though she wasn't sure why. They looked rich, sophisticated, so far beyond her world that Maggie wasn't even sure she could comprehend it.

Nick got out first and held up a hand to help Maggie navigate the stairs. As they deplaned, the trio came over to meet them.

"Darius, Whitney, Gino," Nick said, "This is Maggie."

"Hi." She glanced at Gino. Chubby, happy, with the trademark Andreas dark hair, he was so cute she could have squeezed him. "He's…well, he's so adorable he's breathtaking."

Gino laughed, an airy giggle that warmed Maggie the whole way to her soul. That was what she currently lived for. The day when she'd hear baby giggles. Have someone to guide and love without condition.

"We like him," Darius said, jostling Gino, who jabbered something that contained the word *Dad*.

Whitney stepped forward, glancing at Maggie's tummy, as she took her hands. "You're pregnant."

"Yes. A little over two months to go."

Whitney slid her arm across Maggie's shoulders and began to lead her to the limo. "How exciting for you! Darius and I are talking about having a baby before Gino gets accustomed to being an only child and too spoiled."

Maggie glanced around at the quiet, private airstrip. The area was spotless, silent. There were no other people, no other planes. She'd bet her bottom dollar the Andreas family owned it.

"I don't think there's a snowball's chance in hell that Gino could grow up anything but spoiled."

Whitney laughed merrily. "Oh, you'd be surprised how good I can be at caring for a baby so he doesn't get spoiled."

The driver opened the limo door and Whitney entered with the ease of someone accustomed to luxury, but Maggie glanced around for Nick.

He was at her side in a second. "Everything okay?"

She blew out her breath, feeling a little crazy for having a near panic attack. She'd simply never been around so much luxury before. Her best capris and top felt like rags. Though Nick sensing her distress and racing over eased that odd sensation, it created another.

She hadn't even spoken and he'd come.

Were they getting that much attuned to each other again?

Yes.

The answer came quickly and her heart tumbled in her chest. They'd always had something. A click of recognition. Something.

And she was only kidding herself if she thought she could fight it. Whether she was ready or not, she and Nick were tumbling headfirst into a relationship. She, at least, saw it. Nick—

She glanced around. He'd invited her to meet his family. He'd been by her side every step of the way—

Maybe there was more to this trip than he'd let on? And maybe she was the one lagging behind, not sure she was ready when the truth was it didn't matter if she was ready. She and Nick were a force of nature and if he was falling in love with her again, then she wanted it.

Wanted him.

"Yeah. I'm fine. Just wanted to make sure I wasn't getting into the wrong limo."

He laughed and guided her into the car. "Funny."

She sat on one of the luxurious leather seats. The windows were tinted. The bar discreet. The seat so comfortable she could have happily drifted off into another nap.

As soon as the doors closed and the driver headed toward the front of the vehicle, Darius said, "So, Maggie. Thank you for agreeing to come up and take the notes from our meeting tomorrow morning."

"You're welcome. It's my pleasure." She winced. "Actually I can't wait to see your house." She hoped that hadn't made her sound too much like a penniless bumpkin. "I live five minutes from the beach myself, yet I never get there. I just want one really nice walk on a private beach tomorrow morning."

"Well, that's a given," Whitney said. "If you like, I could come with you."

"No. That's fine. A beach is a beach. I won't wander far enough that I'll overtire or get lost. It's not like I can make any unexpected turns on a shoreline."

Darius laughed. "Sense of humor. I like that."

She smiled, but she also noticed Nick sending Darius some kind of message with his eyes.

Okay. Now this was getting weird. Because Nick had never had much in the way of family when they were dating, she hadn't gone through a screening process. But she had with Josh's family. And she recognized it when she saw it. She might have ostensibly been invited to take a few notes and attend a birthday party, but these people were checking her out.

Oh, God!

These people were checking her out!

The truth of that burst inside her. Something Nick had said caused them to believe there was reason to be worried about her being around him—

Well, she had hurt him. So okay. She got that. But they couldn't be checking her out to make sure she didn't hurt him again. He'd consider that an insult and he'd deck them for that. And he was in on this.

Oh, God!

He *did* have feelings for her.

CHAPTER TEN

As they stepped into the Andreas family's magnificent mansion, people bustled back and forth, in and out and through the entry. Nearly everyone wore black or white and they looked like chess pieces scrambling across the black and white blocks of the foyer floor.

"What's going on?"

Whitney faced Nick with a beaming smile. "Prep for Saturday's party."

"You need a staff for a one-year-old's birthday party?"

"No, silly," Whitney said, taking a clipboard from a woman who had appeared at her side and signing off on something after she read it. "The kids' party is Sunday afternoon. On Saturday night, their parents make big donations in Gino's name to one of three charities we've set up to take gifts. And we thank them with a ball."

Nick watched Maggie's skin grow pasty-white.

He caught her arm. She peeked at him with an expression that totally defied explanation. He couldn't tell if she was scared, sick, shocked...or all three.

"There's a ball?"

"Only about two hundred people," Whitney said, her eyes skimming Maggie's face as she checked her out, obviously seeing the same things Nick had. "It's really not a big deal."

Maggie huffed in a deep breath and laid her hands lightly on her stomach.

Nick nearly had a heart attack. Fear that there was something wrong with her clenched his stomach. He remembered the night she had lost their baby. No warning. Just sudden pain.

"Maggie?"

"I don't…actually, I didn't…well…I packed for the beach."

Relief washed through him as Whitney turned to Darius. "You didn't tell them about the ball?"

He winced. "Sorry. I got everything crossed up."

Whitney faced Maggie with a sunny smile. "No worries. You and I will just go shopping."

"But I—"

"Do it for me. I never get to shop with a girlfriend." Whitney took her arm and began leading her up the stairs. "First, we'll get you settled. You can have a nap or take a long bath or even walk on the beach. When you're ready, we'll shop."

Ten minutes later Maggie was alone in her bedroom, unpacking the few things she'd brought for her stay. The entire room was ivory satin. Chunky bed pillows layered with more delicate throw pillows sat on top of an ivory satin bedspread. The simple hue counteracted the rich cherrywood headboard to make the bed elegantly inviting. Ivory satin drapes were pulled back to reveal a stunning view of the sea.

In front of the bedroom was a sitting room done in soft sage-green. A sage and ivory striped sofa sat by a solid sage Queen Anne chair. Cherrywood tables and an armoire made the room rich, luxurious. The sitting room, bedroom and bath were bigger than her first apartment had been.

Taking out shorts and tank tops, capris and T-shirts and one scrappy pair of jeans, she groaned. There had been no arguing with Whitney about the shopping trip, which in some ways was good because she couldn't exactly wear a scrappy pair of jeans to a ball. But bad because she was about to spend money she didn't have on a dress she'd wear once.

When was she going to get invited to a ball again?

She snorted a laugh just as someone knocked on the door.

Thinking it was the maid with fresh towels or lush scented soap or some kind of expensive, imported chocolate, Maggie sucked it up and said, "Come in," as she walked into the sitting room.

The door opened and Nick entered. "I am so sorry."

Knowing he was talking about not telling her about the ball and deciding to just take it all in stride, Maggie said, "That's okay. I'd have never assumed there'd be a charity ball attached to a one-year-old's birthday party, either."

"Whitney had a child who died. She's very big on charities that involve children."

She pressed her hand to her chest. "Oh, I'm so sorry."

"She's fine. The best thing to do is not mention her past, but she loves to raise money for children's charities. If I'd been on my toes I would have guessed this."

"No harm done."

"Except that you don't have a dress." He stepped closer.

And Maggie noticed something odd.

In a sea of people she didn't know, Nick was the one she did. The one she was comfortable around. And he seemed comfortable with her, too.

"Your sister-in-law has volunteered to rectify the situation."

He laughed.

Maggie smiled. Pinpricks of delight pirouetted across her skin. It was nice to be alone with him, in a neutral environment. He wasn't avoiding making an impression he'd have to live with if the town gossips got a hold of it. She wasn't worried about embarrassing herself in front of people who knew their history. Here where he could be himself, it was clear he really cared about her. She wasn't imagining it because she wanted it so badly.

She remembered the "scoping out" being done by his brother. Though panic tried to rear up, she stopped it in favor of reason. This was what she wanted. Josh was a distant memory. Her marriage to Nick fifteen years ago seemed clearer in her brain than her marriage to Josh. They might have a bumpy road ahead. Some things to iron out. But if he was taking steps to try, then she wanted it, too.

True, it wasn't exactly comfortable to know Nick had brought her here for his family to check her out. It also wasn't fun that she didn't fit in this environment, but she and Nick didn't live in this environment. They lived in a small town, by a beach, with people who said good morning even if they didn't know you and didn't dress in black and white serving uniforms.

If they could get close, admit their feelings, maybe it would hold when they got home?

"I'll be fine."

"Still—" He reached into his pocket and pulled out a money clip. He flipped through the bills until he came upon a credit card, buried in the cash. "Take this. I know Whitney's taste. You'll never be able to afford what she wants you to buy."

This time it wasn't panic that reared up, but disappointment. She wasn't sure which of them she was disappointed in. Him for offering her money—making her feel cheap— or beneath him. Or herself for not having the money to afford a simple party dress—

Well, all right, it wasn't just a dress. It was ball gown for an elite New York event. But she was an adult. She'd worked her whole life. She'd scrimped and saved and her ex-husband had squandered—

She tugged her fingers through her long hair. Yet another gift from her ex-husband. Humiliation in front of someone she wished she could impress. "I have a credit card."

"Yeah, but we don't want to run up any balances."

She laughed. How could she not? He didn't even realize he was talking about them as a "we" a team.

So many emotions tumbled through her. Regret for having married a cretin and for putting up with him for ten years. Fear about what she would be getting herself into if she and Nick really did get together. Pure love for him for being so sweet.

Pure love.

Simple love.

The kind a person only came across once in a life-time.

She almost gasped. It had never left. She had always loved him.

And maybe that was the thing she needed to face. She loved him. There was no "falling" about this. She was already in love.

And he...well, she had no idea what he felt. He might be falling. He might be testing her. His family might be checking her out. Or she could simply be imagining all this.

She pushed away his credit card. She wouldn't take

money, gifts, *anything*, from him until she understood what
was happening between them.

"I'm fine."

He frowned, glanced at his card, then back at her face.
She tried a wobbly smile.

It worked.

He sighed and tucked away his credit card.

"All right. You handle this. But you have my cell phone
if things get dicey."

"They won't."

In the first floor office, Nick flopped on the sofa.

Darius sat at the desk, talking on the phone. He finished the conversation in only a few minutes and rose.
"Drink?"

"No. Too early."

Darius laughed. "Well, that's a good sign. The day
Maggie started you were drinking in the afternoon."

Nick scowled. "It was after five."

"Whatever." Darius dropped to the sofa beside Nick. "I
like her."

"Everybody does."

"A man could do a lot worse."

"Excuse me?"

"Come on. You know you like her. You fawned all over
her in the limo."

Nick gaped at him. "She's pregnant and in a strange
land. I'd do the same for any assistant."

Darius snorted a laugh and rose from the sofa. "If you're
not going to talk about the fun stuff, I have three contracts
here I'd like you to review."

He ambled to the desk and got the contracts, but Nick
couldn't focus. He hadn't fawned all over Maggie. He'd

done a few nice things. He *would have* done the same for any assistant.

Still, he'd given his brother the wrong idea and that could mean he was giving Maggie the wrong idea, too.

That would have to stop.

"So what's the deal with you and Nick?"

Seated in the limo, nearly in the city, having exhausted all potential conversation about where they'd gone to school, their parents, their lack of siblings—except for Maggie's brother who was never around—Maggie lounged against one bench seat while Whitney relaxed against the other.

"You mean aside from the fact that we were married?"

Whitney winced. "Sorry. Darius did tell me the two of you had been married as kids. I wasn't trying to sound like I know nothing at all about you. I know there's history. I'm more interested in the future."

Whitney's forthrightness caused Maggie to frown.

Whitney winced again. "Sorry. I'm a lawyer. Half of what we say sounds like a cross-examination."

"That's okay. I'm not the kind of person to keep secrets, but there really isn't anything to tell. I work for him."

Whitney harrumphed. "You bought that story about them needing you to take minutes?"

"Yes and no." She toyed with the glass of juice Whitney had insisted she drink before they hit the stores. Whitney was the kind of person who inspired honesty, and, being as confused as she was, she could use a friend to talk to. "I think Nick asked me up here so your husband can check me out."

Whitney tapped her long, slim index finger against her lips. "Interesting. They grew up without each other." She smiled. "Of course, you know that. You went to school with Nick, so you know he didn't even know he had brothers. But the thing of it is, last winter once they decided to be brothers for real, they hit the ground running. They really depend on each other. Trust each other. If Nick asked Darius to check you out, there's a reason. A good reason. A big reason."

"Like a test?"

"No, more like the way a guy brings his girl home to his family to see if she fits—"

Fear fizzed through her. Wasn't that the conclusion she'd drawn herself?

"—so that's good."

She shook her head fiercely. "No! It's not good! I *don't* fit! If that's why I'm here I'm toast."

Whitney laughed. "You're not toast. You didn't bring a ball gown. That's all. And apparently Darius's invitation was deficient, not your packing. So we're getting you a dress." She leaned across the space and patted Maggie's hand. "We're getting you one special dress because once you get in the right dress, you'll belong."

"Really?"

"Trust me. My parents were very solidly upper-middle class. Then my dad scored a few really big clients and suddenly we were on Park Avenue. I never thought I'd fit. Especially at my first formal charity event. Then I found the right dress and walked into that ballroom with my head high, knowing I was just as good as everybody else in the room, and—*poof*—I was fine. Sometimes all you need is a little bit of confidence."

"I hope you're right."

Whitney settled into her seat and smiled. "I know I'm right. Plus, the right dress might just be the push Nick needs to admit what he's up to."

"So we're getting this dress to impress Nick?"

The driver opened the door. Gorgeous, sophisticated Whitney stepped out into the hot July sun. This time, she wore white pants and a black shirt with her wide-brimmed black sun hat and black sunglasses.

The picture of sophistication and knowledge, she said, "The right dress can do many things."

That night Maggie felt stupid for spending hundreds of dollars she didn't have on a dress to impress a man. She could say Whitney had been overly persuasive, except she knew in her heart of hearts she desperately wanted Nick to take the next steps. He definitely cared for her. He unconsciously looked out for her. He'd out-and-out offered her money to help her. And he'd asked his brother to check her out.

He had to have some feeling for her. But if she didn't get him to admit it here, where they were just themselves, when they got back to Ocean Palms, where everything was stiff and stilted and too many memories blocked them, he'd go back into his shell and never admit it.

Because she'd packed so sparingly, dinner had been informal in a small dining room that looked out over the ocean.

Darius pulled out Whitney's chair. Nick pulled out Maggie's. She smiled over her shoulder at him. "Thanks."

He returned her smile. "You're welcome."

Maggie's heart swelled like the waves rolling up to the shore. She didn't think this dinner was the be-all and end-all of opportunities for Nick to realize his feelings and be able to voice them. But it was one step in many steps she'd have to take with him this weekend. Everything had to go well.

Darius set his napkin on his lap. "So did you girls have a good day shopping?"

Whitney's eyes sparkled. "The best. Maggie has excellent taste."

Darius laughed, but Nick picked up his water glass and said, "So what happened with the people from London?"

"The group that wants to buy into Andreas Holdings?"

"Yes."

"I shut them down. But we're not the only ones who own Andreas stock. We've got to get to Dad's old secretary before London does. Otherwise they could end up owning one-third of our company."

And with that, Darius broke into a long, detailed explanation of problems that would cause, and Nick listened intently. They talked business through dinner, while Whitney and Maggie discussed how Whitney juggled her life, raising Gino and working. Everything seemed fine. Almost normal. Two couples chitchatting at dinner. Until Darius suggested they retire to the game room to play pool or cards.

Suddenly Nick glanced at her, glanced at the door and said, "I think I'll just go to my suite. In fact, I think I should walk Maggie to her suite, too."

Happiness burst inside her. He wanted to be alone with her. If that wasn't a good sign, she didn't know what was. "Yes. I am a little tired."

He took her elbow and led her through the maze of halls in the downstairs and finally up the spiral staircase to her room.

At the door, he met her gaze. "Can I come in for a second?"

Nerves and joy attacked her simultaneously. "Yes. Sure."

"Great."

He opened the door for her and she walked into the sitting room.

He pointed at the sofa. "Have a seat."

She smiled. "Uh, since this is my room, isn't it me who's supposed to say that?"

He chuckled. His eyes crinkled at the corners when he smiled and Maggie's heart sang. He was the older, wiser version of the boy she had loved, but she loved him every bit as fiercely as she'd loved Nick Roebuck. If he was here, in her room, to spend time with her, to tell her he was beginning to have feelings or even just to kiss her again to test the waters, she wanted it.

She facilitated it. She sat on the sofa instead of the chair so he could sit beside her.

He did.

Her heart thumping in her chest, she set her hands on her lap to still them.

"Maggie, there's something I have to tell you."

"Yes?" She pried her nervous hands apart, giving him the chance to take them.

He didn't, but he did gaze into her eyes. "By now I guess you've figured out that I didn't just bring you here to take notes."

Telling her pounding heart to calm down, she smiled. "I'd have to be pretty thick to have missed the signs."

He winced. "Darius isn't very good at being sneaky."

She laughed. "No."

"I'm amazed he didn't tell Whitney what was going on."

"Don't underestimate Whitney. She has her suspicions."

He laughed nervously. "Right." He sucked in a breath.

"Anyway, since there's no point in hiding this anymore, I've decided to just come right out and tell you what's going on."

As a prelude to telling her he loved her, or even was only interested in her again, that left a lot to be desired. He'd been a lot more romantic as an eighteen-year-old.

"Sunday and Monday, I talked about you at length with my brothers. Cade, my younger brother, suggested that it was time I see the truth."

Her hands shivered with the need to take his. Her tongue nearly said the words he was taking so long to say. She had to clamp her teeth together to stay silent.

"I need to move here to New York to take some responsibility from Darius. And I'd like to make you my general manager of Andreas Manufacturing."

She managed to prevent her mouth from dropping open, but for thirty seconds silence reigned.

Finally Nick broke it. "I thought you'd be pleased."

"Yes!" She bounced off the sofa, desperately trying to shift her brain to work mode and to blink away the tears flooding her eyes. But frustration and disbelief rose up in her. He'd kissed her. He was attracted to her. Whether he knew it or not he'd brought her home to meet his family—

She spun to face him. She couldn't quell the disbelief that roared through her and demanded clarification. "This has all been about a job?"

"Not just any job. I want you to take over my company. This is a big step for me. For both of us." He paused. "What did you think it was about?"

She swallowed, turned away again. Dear God, if she cried, she would kick her own butt.

"Maggie?"

When she wouldn't face him, he put his hands on her shoulders. The warmth of them seeped through her simple T-shirt, and tried to warm her heart. He might not love her but he cared about her enough to make sure she had a really good job. More, though, he now trusted her.

He turned her around. "You wanted this to be about us?"

She wouldn't look at him.

"There is no us." His voice was a soft whisper. "There can't be an us."

She swallowed.

"I loved you fifteen years ago."

Definitely unable to meet his gaze for this, she mumbled, "And you're still attracted to me now."

"That's physical." He chuckled sadly. "I'm not sure that's ever going to go away. But you're right. It's always been about more than sex with us. You were the one person I was absolutely positive believed in me."

For that she caught his gaze, searched his dark, dark eyes. "I did."

He shook his head. "No. You didn't. You left. You might as well have said you didn't believe I would make it unless I got help from my dad. You broke that trust."

She frowned, confused that he was laying all this at her feet as if he'd had no part in things. "I was young and exhausted. I'd just lost a baby. I wasn't thinking about trust. Only about need. About you and your mom going without—"

"I needed you. Not money."

His voice was soft, calm. But anger had begun to brew inside Maggie. The arrogant confidence in his tone trembled through her like the first shakes of an earthquake. He might not have been the one to leave, but he was far from innocent.

She didn't stop the fury that seeped into her tone when she confronted him. "Oh, yeah. You needed me? So why didn't you try to find me? Why did you simply let me go? I was home for a week before I left for university. Yet, you never came after me. Never once recognized I might not have been in a good enough emotional state to make the choice I'd made. You simply let me go."

"Maggie, no man goes after a woman who doesn't have faith in him. Especially not the one person he always believed was his number one supporter."

"You think I don't have faith in you?" Shaking her head, she sniffed a laugh. "When I needed a job, who did I come to? When I was pregnant, alone, abandoned by the husband who simply walked away for greener pastures, who did I come to? I didn't think we'd get back together. I gave no thought to the fact that we might still have chemistry. I was in trouble and I knew the one person in the world who could help me was you…and that's who I trusted. Who I came to. You."

The truth of that hit Nick in the gut and totally disarmed him. "You came to me because you knew I could help?"

"I might have come for a job, but it was because I knew for sure I could depend on you to help me. You were always the only one I knew I could depend on."

Her admission didn't change the fact that she'd left him. But she was right. He'd never gone after her. He'd let his blasted pride stop him. Pride so thick it had taken him years to grow up and out of it. Still, he wasn't that boy anymore and she wasn't that frightened girl. She was a smart, successful woman, who when she'd fallen on hard times had turned to him. And he was a smart successful man, who, when she'd come, couldn't turn her away.

"Wow."

"I'm sick of paying for something that happened fifteen years ago," Maggie said, her voice thick with tears. "I'm sick of thinking about it, talking about it—"

"So am I." Hands already on her shoulders, Nick yanked her to him. The truth of the present didn't merely override the events of the past, it obliterated them. They were adults. Two different people. Two people who'd both made mistakes. Two people who could only find longed-for redemption with each other.

He pressed his mouth to hers and kissed her the way he'd wanted to kiss her when she'd first walked into his office. He slanted his mouth over hers, taking, not asking, not caring that he might be rough or crude. He'd waited fifteen long years to kiss her again. And he intended to indulge, enjoy.

She opened her mouth on a gurgled sound of pleasure that seeped into his skin and set fire to his blood. He couldn't get enough of the feel of her, the taste of her. When his hands skimmed down her arms and back up again, he redirected them to her waist. He cruised the slight indentation, then shifted upward until he met her breast.

Her breathing changed. So did his. The fire in his blood became an inferno of need that totally shut off his thought process. This was what he wanted, what they both wanted.

And it was time.

But Maggie pulled away. "No. Wait. Stop." She gulped in air, obviously trying to get her bearings. "Everything's happening so fast."

It was true. Even through his passionate haze he could see her fear. And why not? They might have been lovers fifteen years ago, married fifteen years ago, but they were now interacting as two new people. And the new person he'd become barely bore any resemblance to the boy she'd loved.

He stepped back.

She blinked up at him. "So now what?"

"I'm not sure." He wasn't. He'd never even considered a permanent relationship with any woman but Maggie. Part of him wanted to pick up where they'd left off. The other part knew that couldn't happen. No one can really pretend fifteen years hadn't happened. Worse, Nick Andreas didn't have permanent relationships.

"We can't just ride off into the sunset."

"No. We can't." He peered over at her, chuckled. "Maggie, I'm way different from the guy you married."

"I know."

"I've done my share of running around."

"I guessed that."

"The thing is…I'm not sure I can settle down."

Her head tilted. Then she laughed. "Maybe that's our problem. Maybe we look at each other and don't see a potential partner, we see instant marriage. Maybe what we need to do is pull back, sort of start over." She walked over and slid her hands around his neck. "Actually date."

"We never did date."

"No. We didn't."

"We went right from friends to lovers to a married couple in a few weeks."

She kissed him lightly. "Exactly."

He slid his hands around her waist. "So, what do we do?"

"Well, I'm going to kiss you good-night and you're going to leave."

He frowned. "I'm not sure I like this."

"Which is probably why we skipped the dating step." She kissed him again. "You can be very persuasive."

One more kiss.

"But good night."

CHAPTER ELEVEN

Two minutes before nine o'clock on Saturday morning, Maggie found the downstairs office and slipped inside, trying to appear cool, calm and efficient. She was here to be an assistant. So what if she could have easily made love with Nick the night before? So what if she and Nick hadn't just cleared the air, they'd cleared a path to be together? She was just about certain neither one of them wanted to announce that to his brothers. At least not until they themselves understood what they were doing.

Plus, she still had to take notes.

She knew her calm attitude was the right choice when Nick said a pleasant, but restrained, "Good morning," and introduced her to his brother Cade—a typical Andreas with dark hair, broad shoulders and shrewd dark eyes.

As soon as she was settled, Darius started the meeting.

The morning passed quickly in a flurry of discussions and the kind of arguments only brothers could have. Maggie was amazed at how close they'd become, considering that Whitney had told her they'd only decided to be brothers for real the past January.

They broke for lunch and then picked up where they left off for another two hours of discussion.

When the meeting was over, Maggie went to her room,

intending to begin inputting the minutes in her laptop but she fell asleep. She didn't awaken until someone knocked on her door. Fearing it was Nick, she fixed her hair when she passed a mirror and raced to the sitting room.

"Come in," she said as she opened the door, only to find Whitney on the other side.

She held out a simple gold necklace with a small diamond pendant and diamond earrings. "I brought these for you to wear."

Maggie gasped. "I couldn't."

"Don't worry." She smiled. "You're only borrowing them. Besides, you have to. If you wear anything else with that dress, you'll overpower it. These are perfect."

Staring at them, Maggie had to admit they were perfect. And she did want to look good for Nick. "Okay."

"Okay." Whitney turned away, then faced Maggie again. "And breathe. Darius said the meeting went well, you were a star and Nick told them he'd already given you the general manager's job."

"Really?" In everything that had happened, she'd forgotten about the job, about the fact that Nick wanted to move to New York.

"Really. You're set. So just relax and enjoy."

When Whitney was gone, Maggie pressed a hand to her stomach. Relax? Enjoy? They weren't even officially dating and already she had to face a problem. She'd finally, finally come home and he was leaving. Moving to New York.

Ten minutes after the official start time of the ball, Nick headed for Maggie's suite. He knew what he was doing. When he and Maggie walked into that ballroom together tonight, they'd be a couple. But that was good. He didn't want to give himself any way out or any way to finagle himself and Maggie into something less than what she needed. She wanted to date for real. To give them a real shot. And he agreed.

Still, nerves jangled. His tie felt too tight. Hell, his skin felt too tight.

Two seconds before Nick would have knocked on Maggie's suite door, she opened it. The scent that was so uniquely Maggie greeted him first, nearly paralyzing him with wicked thoughts. Then he looked at her.

Her long red hair had been pinned up in a bundle of curls. Some hung loose and danced along her neck, pulling Nick's gaze there, then to her shoulders. The sleeves of her pale yellow gown draped to her biceps, leaving her shoulders and chest bare, taking his gaze to her breasts. They peeked out over the satiny yellow material, but not a lot. Just a peek. Just enough to whet a man's appetite and maybe even make him thank his maker.

He took a step back. The gown skimmed her trim, toned body and glided over her baby bump. It hugged her hips and caressed her thighs and fell to the floor with a loose grace that made it all at once sexy and elegant.

"Wow."

She smiled sheepishly. "Your sister-in-law has good taste."

Though he let himself be a little mesmerized, something inside his gut told him to stop. To hold back. Because he was sure it was the playboy inside him, he ignored it. He'd loved this woman and she was working her way back into his life. This was the thing he could do with Maggie that he hadn't been able to do with any other woman. Be smitten. Charmed. Hypnotized. It was the first step to being able to commit and he told his panicky feeling to settle down, and he just let himself enjoy.

"No. You have one hell of a body. I think you could make sack cloth and ashes look good."

He held out his arm and she slid her hand into the crook of his elbow.

"Shall we?"

She drew in a quick breath. "Yeah. I'm as ready as I'll ever be."

"You'll dazzle them."

"Right. I'm a small-town girl who really wasn't all that successful in the big city. I was lucky to get a job with you, Nick."

Her voice was so soft, so serious, that he stopped. Guilt welled inside his chest. They'd screwed up their lives royally. Her by leaving. Him by letting her go. Not finding her once he'd refused the money. Not realizing she'd been in no state to make their big decision. They'd talked this all out the night before. He wouldn't let it hold her prisoner.

"We were lucky to find each other."

As soon as the words were out of his mouth, he realized how true they were, but that itchy little shadow of doubt nudged at him again. Again, he ignored it.

They glided down the spiral staircase into the front foyer where they were greeted by Darius and Whitney. Dressed in a pale blue strapless gown, Whitney was the kind of beautiful that could stop traffic. But to Nick she didn't hold a candle to Maggie.

"You look fabulous!" Whitney said, bussing a kiss on Maggie's cheek. "I told you you would be fine."

Maggie laughed. Darius kissed her cheek, told her she looked fantastic and more or less handed her and Nick off into the ballroom.

Within three seconds Cade was at their side. He pulled at the collar of his white tuxedo shirt. "I hate these things."

Nick laughed. "They're not so bad."

"Not to you, Mr. Party Guy." He yanked on his collar again. "I live on a ranch, spend time on oil rigs. I don't do things like this."

Once again, Nick felt a nudge of something that made him feel odd, uncomfortable. Cade hadn't necessarily meant anything by his comment. But it gave Nick that too-tight skin feeling again. He was well-known for dating starlets, sophisticates and even a princess or two. He didn't commit. Yet, here he was with a pregnant woman—a woman he shouldn't hurt—

That's when he understood. The feeling racing through him wasn't about his fear that he couldn't commit, it was the knowledge that he shouldn't even try this unless he was sure. Because if he wasn't, Maggie was the one who would be hurt.

But, knee-deep in the conversation with Cade, Maggie laughed. "Well, if it's any consolation you look great. I'll bet all the available women are salivating at the possibility of dancing with you."

"Was that an offer?"

Maggie froze, but Nick stepped between her and Cade so quickly she wouldn't have had a chance to answer anyway. "She's spoken for."

"So what? She's not dancing."

Taking her hand, Nick turned to the dance floor. "She is now."

They twirled out onto the floor in a waltz. Her gown flowed around them. He caught her gaze and she smiled at him. This was right. This was what he wanted. He twirled her until they reached the French doors, then he twirled her one more time, taking them out to an empty terrace.

Silver moonlight enveloped them. Her skin glowed. Her eyes sparkled. Contentment settled over him. They moved around the terrace to the waltz, gazing into each other's eyes. Happy. When the song ended, Maggie stepped fully into his embrace, but before Nick could kiss her, Cade appeared in the doorway.

"Darius sent me to find you. Dinner's about to be served. We're on the head table with him."

Nick took Maggie's hand and led her to the door. Cade slapped his back. "I hope you brought your checkbook because I'm not even going to tell you how much Whitney hit me up for."

Nick laughed, too. *This* he understood. "My checkbook's at home. But I was thinking of doing a wire transfer anyway."

Cade laughed. "Always one-upping everybody."

A weird sensation stole through him. It was as if Cade's words turned him back into Nick Andreas. "I don't one-up."

"Of course, you do." Cade casually headed into the ballroom. "We all do. It's part of being an Andreas."

They found the head table and Nick pulled out Maggie's chair. Dinner was served. Whitney made a sweet plea for money from the nearby podium. And the band began to play again.

A few minutes later, Darius returned to the table where Nick and Maggie sat, lingering over dessert.

"Cade, Whitney and I are going upstairs to say goodnight to Gino. Would you like to come along?"

Maggie all but jumped out of her chair. "I'd love to."

Nick laughed. "I'd also love to."

They met Cade and Whitney in the foyer, eased up the circular stairway and back a long hall to the nursery. Darius opened the door.

Baby cries, toddler shouts and laughter poured out like the roar of a lion. Chaos reigned.

"Come in!" Working hard to be heard above the noise, Gino's nanny, Liz, a pretty blonde who looked to be about twenty, motioned them inside.

Whitney and Maggie entered first, then Cade and Darius.

Nick followed his brothers in. Two little boys about Gino's age played on a mat on the floor. Three little girls who looked to be a year or two older than Gino sat at the small plastic table and chairs having a tea party. A baby lay in a bassinette.

"Who are all these kids?"

"Play date," Liz answered simply. "When the parents party, I volunteer to hold a play date for Gino."

Whitney laughed. "I tell her she's crazy."

"But the kids love it," Liz insisted. "They always sense when their parents are out for the evening and it makes them unhappy. This way they feel like they're part of things."

Nick noticed Cade looking uneasily at the three little girls currently arguing over a teapot, as if the noise of their argument slithered like a rattlesnake along his skin.

He felt the same weird pressure building up in him. Kids were cute. He was around them all the time at his mom's daycare. He'd simply never gotten this close to them. He was always kind of looking at them through a doorway. Or waving as he drove past his mom carrying one. He wasn't accustomed to being with kids who weren't old enough to play Wiffle Ball.

Liz continued talking. "After they've run out of steam, I read a story and they fall asleep."

"Maybe we should take Gino into another room to say good-night?" Whitney suggested, pointing to a door to the right.

Darius scooped Gino off the mat, but he immediately leaned out of Darius's arms, begging Nick to take him.

Nick beamed and realized that his former thought process was incorrect. He *had* gotten very close to a kid who wasn't old enough to play Wiffle Ball. Gino. He adored this little boy. He couldn't define or describe the feelings that welled up in him every time Gino sought him out. Or hugged him. Or gave him one of those sloppy kisses only a baby could give. He wasn't quite sure why the other kids scared him, except maybe there were so many of them.

They trooped toward the master bedroom door, but suddenly the baby in the bassinette began to yelp. The tea party girls' fight intensified. The two abandoned boys on the mat burst into wails.

Everybody but Liz and Maggie froze.

"I've got this," Liz insisted.

But Maggie pulled the baby from the bassinette. "I'll take him. You settle the others and I'll bring him back when we bring Gino."

Liz said a quick, "Okay, thanks," as she headed over to break up the tea party scuffle.

They walked through the sophisticated brown and aqua master bedroom into the sitting room in front of it. Nick sat on the sofa with Gino, who playfully slapped his face.

"I think you have too much energy to go to sleep."

Gino yelped.

Everybody laughed. Cade snagged him from Nick's lap. "Hey, kid. I'm going downstairs to see if I can't find a little entertainment tonight with a willing woman. So I'm going to kiss you and hug you and bug out of here."

"That's not something you tell a baby," Darius scolded.

But Whitney laughed. "It's fine." She turned to Cade. "But next year it won't be."

Cade said, "Yes, ma'am," kissed Gino's cheek noisily and handed him back to Nick before he left the room.

Nick also gave him a quick kiss. The nursery noise had fallen off to almost nothing, which probably meant story time was in progress. He wasn't surprised when Darius hoisted Gino off his lap.

"I hear Liz reading. It's best for Gino to already be in his crib for this."

Nick rose. "Right."

Whitney faced Maggie. "You can bring little Bruce in, too, now."

"Can I have two more minutes?"

Whitney's eyes softened with love, but something puckered in Nick's chest. In a few short weeks, Maggie would give birth to a little one like that.

Whitney and Darius took Gino into the nursery and Nick rose from the sofa. He walked over to Maggie.

"Let me see Bruce."

She handed the baby over with a smile and Nick looked down at the kid. Because he was a baby, just a little younger than Gino had been when he came into their lives, Nick expected to feel the rich, deep emotion he'd felt the first time he'd held Gino, but he felt nothing. No surge of love. Or joy. Or even slight happiness.

He supposed it made perfect sense. He loved Gino. He was his blood. He could do no wrong. Nick didn't have that connection to any of the other kids here so he didn't feel the love.

It wasn't a big deal. It certainly wasn't something he'd even mention now that he'd figured it out. But even as he thought that, his gaze fell to Maggie's growing belly. And suddenly he realized this horrible feeling wasn't just about some nameless kids attending his half brother's birthday party.

What if he didn't feel anything for Maggie's baby?

CHAPTER TWELVE

WHEN they returned to Ocean Palms, Maggie could feel the change in Nick. He was lighter. Happier. So much like the old Nick that sometimes it was hard to believe fifteen years had passed since they were married as kids.

With the bid in, her training period began, and so did their dating. They went to movies, concerts, took walks on the beach. Though Nick began spending two days a week at Andreas Holdings headquarters, they never discussed his moving to New York. And soon Maggie realized why. He wouldn't talk about anything permanent because no matter how much she loved him or how much he seemed to love her, there were no guarantees. So he wouldn't make any specific plans. That way if things didn't work out between them, moving away could be his fallback position.

Which was fine. Great actually. If things didn't work out between them personally, she'd still have a job and he could get far enough away that each could get over the breakup. But Maggie was supremely confident things would work out. She and Nick had always fit like two puzzle pieces. And they definitely still had sizzle.

Recognizing the change in their situation, her dad shamelessly asked Nick for help getting in his hay. Since he was spending half his weekend at the farm anyway,

Charlie figured he might as well work. And Nick happily agreed.

Friday in the second week of August, when the air was thick with late summer heat, the town kids chatted about going back to school, and her training period was coming to an end, Maggie arrived at work feeling like the boss.

Driving up to her private parking space in her shiny new red SUV, the work and rewards finally came together for her. Nick was returning from two days in New York and she'd been running the show for over a month. People respected her. She knew the ropes. She had some experience, not just theory.

"Good morning, Janette," she said, smiling at *her* new assistant, a thirty-something single mom, who wasn't afraid to get her hands dirty or dig in and do difficult work.

"Good morning, Maggie. Mail is open and on your desk."

Maggie said thanks and breezed through to her office. She plopped into the chair and immediately began returning phone calls.

Though Nick was supposed to fly home that morning and come to Andreas Manufacturing in the afternoon, he strode into the office about twenty minutes after she did. His hair was still wet from the shower. He wore jeans and a big sloppy T-shirt. He walked around the desk, spun her chair around, leaned in and kissed her.

Delight danced through her. "Thought you were flying back this morning."

He kissed her again. "I flew home last night."

"At?"

He winced. "About midnight. We finished up at ten and by the time I got packed and to the airstrip, it was... late."

She laughed.

"Hey, I missed you."

"I missed you, too."

And she hadn't forgotten that tonight was supposed to be *the* night. They'd had several close calls with making love, but for one reason or another it had never actually happened. Pretty soon she'd be too big and too tired to even consider it and she wanted it to be special, perfect. So when he'd left on Tuesday, she'd promised and he'd made her pinky swear that tonight would be the night.

"My dad's driving to Ohio today."

"Oh, yeah?"

"Yep. Gonna go see Charlie Jr."

"Really?"

"So now we don't have to worry about asking his permission for me to spend the weekend."

He laughed. "It's just like when we were kids."

Framing his face with her hands, she laughed. "Not quite. This time we know what we're getting into."

A shadow passed across his face. Quickly. But she'd seen it. Something serious was troubling him. "What's wrong?"

He pulled away. "Nothing."

"There's something."

He shook his head. "Yeah, we have to work eight hours before we can go home."

Though his answer was meant to reassure her, he was having doubts. Big or small, it sent a warning spiraling through her.

She told herself to forget it. They'd make love tonight and maybe another time or two over the next week, but soon she'd have to abstain. She didn't want to lose this chance by pushing him to talk about something that might be nothing.

* * *

At five o'clock, Nick listened for the sounds of Janette leaving. Drawers closed. Her computer wound down. She popped her head inside the office.

"See you on Monday, Maggie." She glanced at him. "See you Monday, Nick."

Maggie said, "Good night."

Nick smiled and waved.

One. Two. Three.

The door closed.

He leaped off the sofa. "I thought she'd never leave."

Leaning back in the tall chair behind the desk, Maggie laughed. "It's actually two minutes till five." She rose. "You're impatient."

"Not arguing that." He grabbed his keys and cell phone from the coffee table, motioned for her to precede him. "Let's go."

"Wait!" She laughed. "We haven't even discussed logistics yet."

His brow furrowed. "Logistics?"

"Do you want to come with me to my house while I pack a bag so you can drive me to your house?"

"Yes." Sheesh. He was a moron. If he were any more eager, he'd take her right here on the sofa.

He sucked in a breath. Smiled. "We'll both drive to your dad's house. You can pack a bag and leave your car, and life will be good."

"Great."

She drove to the farm and he followed a safe distance behind her. In the car, he reminded himself that she was a pregnant woman. Perhaps not physically delicate, but certainly not agile. And let's not forget emotional. Tonight had to be special.

He pulled the Porsche in beside her new SUV, jumped out and headed up the porch steps like a calm, sane man.

Walking into the dark foyer, he assumed she was upstairs and he went into the kitchen for a glass of water. But he stopped dead in the doorway. Her dad sat at the kitchen table, head in his hands.

"What's up?"

Maggie sent him a pleading look, as Charlie said, "I can't go."

"You can't?"

"He's missing Vicki."

"Not just missing Vicki," Charlie corrected. "I'm having trouble with the whole situation. Every time I get to the highway, I remember driving to Charlie Jr.'s with her and somehow or another that takes me back in time to when I found her."

Nick eased over to the table, pulled out a chair and sat. "I think that's probably normal."

Charlie dragged his fingers through his hair. "I was so lonely after your mom died and Vicki walked into my life and suddenly I wasn't alone anymore."

Nick's gaze shot to Maggie's face. The way Charlie was talking it was as if Maggie hadn't even existed. He could see from the question in her eyes that Maggie felt it, too.

Still, she patted her dad's arm and said, "I know. Vicki coming into your life was a good thing."

"And Charlie Jr., too." He shook his head. "Man, she loved that baby. She was such a great mom."

Maggie stiffened. She said, "Yes, she was," but Nick could see the hurt on her face.

"She loved doing school things with him, loved taking him to the beach. And bake? Every time he sneezed she baked him cookies."

Maggie swallowed, but she quickly pulled herself together and snuggled against her dad's shoulder, comforting him. "I know. She was great."

But Nick wasn't a daughter struggling to comfort her dad, and he knew the truth. Vicki hadn't been a great mother. At least not in Nick's memory. She might have been mother of the year to her own child, but the child who'd come to her by default, Maggie, had largely gone ignored. Maggie had felt like an outsider in her own home. Worse, her father had never noticed. And maybe Vicki hadn't, either. They were both nice people, good people. Especially Charlie. He wouldn't deliberately ignore anyone. Yet, he hadn't noticed that his second wife had never taken to the child from his first marriage.

Maggie rose to get her dad a drink and Nick glanced at her protruding stomach. Fear skittered through him. He felt nothing for her baby. Except maybe jealousy. Nick might have been the first man to make Maggie pregnant, but another man had given her the child she'd hold. Another man had given her the baby she'd become a mother to. How could he not be jealous?

How could he guarantee he wouldn't be like Vicki, not quite able to love her child?

How could he say he wouldn't unintentionally hurt Maggie's baby the way Vicki had hurt Maggie?

Nick stayed another twenty minutes and helped Maggie start supper. But when she asked him to set the table, he rubbed his hand across the back of his neck. "I think I'm going to head home. Let you and your dad have some privacy."

She nodded, walked over and brushed his lips with a kiss. "As soon as he's sleeping, I'll come over."

Nick smiled before he left, but the seeds of discord that had been growing inside him had begun to sprout into full-blown doubt. No matter how much he loved Maggie, if he put her baby into the same kind of home life that she'd had, she'd never forgive him.

Hell, he'd never forgive himself.

He had to figure out a way to fix this.

Maggie finally got her dad into bed at about nine. She hastily packed a bag, showered, dressed in a pretty, airy sundress and headed to Nick's.

As was her practice, she didn't knock. She parked her SUV in the garage beneath the house and headed up the stairway into the butler's pantry and to the kitchen.

"Nick?"

"I'm out here."

She turned to face the French doors, which were open. But the deck light wasn't on. Confused, she set her bag on a close counter and walked outside.

"Hey."

He didn't turn from the railing. "Hey."

So she met him there, mimicking his position by leaning her forearms on the wooden rail and looking out into the darkness. "What's up?"

"The stars are pretty tonight."

She glanced up. "They are." The stars were bright, the ocean nothing more than a comfortable roar a hundred yards or so beyond Nick's house. Only the white foam of an occasional wave was visible in the darkness.

Nick stayed silent and the odd, unnamed fear she'd had that morning resurrected. She'd seen the shadow cross his face while they were chatting in the office. He'd also left her to deal with her dad alone. Normally he stayed around. Talked her dad through his sadness. Tonight, he'd gone.

She bumped his shoulder. "So why'd you leave me all alone with my dad?"

He still didn't look at her, didn't say anything and the unnamed fear took hold, took meaning. All along it had seemed too good to be true that they could pick up where they had left off. And she knew—she just knew—he was having second thoughts. Making love the first time had taken them from friends to a married couple. It had been a lightning-fast change. No chance to think things through or look back.

And today they were going to make love again. For the first time in this portion of their relationship. Undoubtedly he knew there'd be no turning back. And maybe he wasn't ready?

She eased away from the railing. "If you don't want me to stay—"

He pivoted to face her. "No. God. No. I'm sorry." He scrubbed his hand across his mouth. "It's just—I just…" He sucked in a breath. "I've been having some weird thoughts lately."

"What kind of weird thoughts?"

"You know how I—you—" He stopped, huffed out a breath. "All that talk about Vicki being a good mom tonight floored me."

"She was a good mother."

"To Charlie Jr."

She laughed as relief rippled through her. "I told you all that was resolved."

He took her upper arms in his warm hands and caught her gaze. "That's not what I saw on your face tonight."

"A momentary lapse."

"Really?" He studied her eyes. "Because it's been fifteen years since you and Vicki supposedly found your footing, yet thinking about your childhood hurt you."

"A bit." She might as well admit it. Nick had been her best friend through that time. He knew how alone she'd felt. How abandoned. She might not have thought about it in a while, but being home had brought a lot of it back. And, tonight, her dad's words had cut like a knife. "But I've decided to treat it as only a momentary lapse. She might not have been there for me. But she had been for Charlie Jr." Unconsciously she rubbed her hands along her swollen tummy. "But I now understand why it happened. I wasn't her blood child."

She stopped herself because the color had drained from Nick's face and his gaze had fallen to her stomach.

And suddenly his fears made sense.

He didn't love her baby. Didn't *want* to love her baby.

"Oh, my God."

She turned to go but Nick stopped her. "Wait! Wait!" He shook his head in regret. "It's not what you think. Things are just confusing for me right now."

She searched his eyes. "How confusing?"

"I'm involved with a woman who's pregnant with another man's child. But I've also seen the life you've led, being that child, the child from a different relationship. I didn't just see Vicki ignore you. I saw the end result. I saw you cry." He raked his fingers through his hair. "I know how you hurt."

She stepped back, out of his reach. "You don't want my baby."

It was a statement, not a question.

"I don't want to *hurt* your baby and I feel—"

"Feel what?" she demanded as the blood in her veins chilled to just above freezing. She now had proof Nick didn't want her baby. Nick Andreas never stammered. He didn't get confused. He always knew what he wanted. If he thought he was confused now, it was because he was arguing with the answer he already knew.

"That's just it. I don't know."

She squeezed her eyes shut.

"I'm afraid we're going to do to your baby what Vicki did to you."

She took another two steps back. "I'm not. I'm not even close to fearing that. You know why? Because I know you and I know the huge capacity you have to love. If you're worried that you can't love my baby…it's because you don't, because you know you won't."

She spun away and headed for the French doors. She grabbed her overnight bag and raced down the stairs.

"Wait! Maggie!" Nick was on her heels. "Damn it, Maggie! I thought you said we could talk about anything. We have to talk about this."

She jumped into her SUV. "We just did."

And Nick watched her go. Once again, she'd made a decision for them. He wanted to talk. She ran. And maybe that was what was fundamentally wrong with their relationship.

CHAPTER THIRTEEN

"LET me get this straight. You're working on a Monday?"

Nick rolled his eyes and headed for the silver coffee service in his New York office. "Maggie's trained now. She doesn't need me."

"She's about to give birth. I think she needs you."

"She has six weeks."

"So you're here?"

"Yes. Full-time."

Darius just stared at him. But Nick gave him a look. The look. The one that said *don't cross this boundary*.

Darius shrugged. "Fine." He tossed a stack of papers on Nick's desk. "That's the email trail for my discussion with the group of private investors in London who want to buy into Andreas Holdings. They know there's another shareholder."

"And you want me to...do what?"

"Just familiarize yourself with the backstory. Because if we don't find that shareholder before the people in London do, we may be going to war."

Darius left and Nick settled down at his desk. Picking up the papers Darius had left him, he forced himself not to think about Maggie. Half of him understood why she'd balked, been appalled, about his worry over not being able to love her baby. The other half was angry. He was only human. He hadn't asked for the weird feelings, for the fear. Yet, she'd acted as if he'd calmly, rationally decided not to love her child.

He ran his hands down his face. She'd been hurt.

Hell, he'd been hurt!

But he'd tried to call her. Had tried to see her. And she wouldn't answer the phone or see him. Maybe that's why he hadn't gone after her the first time. She was stubborn.

Pain rippled through him at the thought. She wasn't stubborn...well, maybe a little... She was hurt. He knew she was hurt and she wouldn't let him help her, wouldn't let him try to fix this.

Of course, he'd been the one to make the problem.

Which took him back to the fact that he hadn't asked for his feelings.

He just had them.

He still had them.

And maybe she was right not to want to see him. Maybe there was no way to work this out.

The only thing he could do was work. Get his mind off this. So he put his attention on the email trail Darius wanted him to read and started in. He worked until five o'clock, then realized he hadn't even taken a break for lunch. Without a word to anyone, he left Andreas Holdings and went straight to Darius's penthouse apartment. Normally he'd stay at the house in Montauk, but he wasn't ready for that yet. Whitney would know he and Maggie had split. If she didn't know today, she'd know soon because she and Maggie had become friends. And then Nick would face a million questions that he'd prefer not to answer right now.

How would he explain to Whitney, lovable Whitney, who'd lost a baby, that he didn't have an ounce of feelings for Maggie's little one? He'd tried. He'd honest-to-God tried to feel something for Maggie's baby. But when he did, the only emotion that registered was horrible jealousy. Maggie had no trouble carrying this baby. But she'd lost theirs. He wasn't pointing fingers. He knew nature was nature. Maggie was not at fault. So, he supposed he was railing at nature. Angry with fate. Disgusted with destiny. Why had his baby died?

A million emotions washed through him as he entered the penthouse. Rich buttery hardwood floors and a sky-line view of the city greeted him as he entered. He barely noticed them. One minute he shook with rage. The next he was a puddle of sadness, of loss.

He grabbed a bottle of twelve-year-old Scotch and headed for the TV room, where he planned to drink himself to sleep.

It took two weeks before Maggie stopped crying herself to sleep. Nick no longer came to the plant. He stayed in New York. Every Friday morning, he called Janette who filled him in on any phone calls or correspondence that needed his attention. But he never spoke to Maggie.

She could think that he was still angry and didn't want anything to do with her, but she had a feeling that, like her, he knew talking would only be painful and slow their recovery from their breakup.

Which meant he wanted to recover. He wasn't coming home so there'd be no risk that seeing her would make him long for what they'd had. What they had was deficient. He really and truly believed he couldn't love her child and if he couldn't love her child, then there was no future for them. Because he was right. She would not let her child be raised by a parent who couldn't love him.

Him.

Her baby could be a boy. And if it was he would need

a male influence. Not someone who loved his mom, but didn't love him. But someone to teach him. Someone to guide him along the road to being a man. She'd learned firsthand from Vicki that if the same sex parent had no interest in a child, there'd be no teaching. There'd be no bonding. And that would leave a huge hole. A void. Her child would live a loneliness that couldn't be described.

She wouldn't do that to her baby.

So she spent the next three weeks telling herself that Nick walking away had been the right thing.

That Friday, she hadn't even watched the door hoping Nick would stroll through, as she had the first few Fridays of her tenure as general manager. She didn't linger until six, thinking he might pop in after he thought she was gone, so that she could catch him, and if nothing else see him.

She was beyond all that. Strong now. Getting ready for her baby.

As she drove home, a storm began rolling in. Dark clouds gathered, filling the blue sky with inky blackness.

Dressed in a suit and a crisp white shirt, her dad glanced over her head as she walked inside. She could see from the worried expression that clouded his eyes that he didn't like the look of the sky.

"Are you sure you don't mind me going?"

She set her briefcase on the kitchen table and smiled. "Positive."

This time, the expression on his face said he didn't believe her. He shrugged out of his jacket. "You know what? I don't really need to go to bereavement group tonight."

"You do!" Maggie crossed the room, picked up his jacket and handed it to him. "I'm fine."

He laughed. "Okay. Okay. I get it. I'm a mess without the group. I'm going."

Walking across the kitchen to the door, he shrugged into his jacket again. One foot on the back porch he hesitated. "Wow. That storm's going to be a beaut."

She glanced at the dark, angry clouds. "You know what? I think you'd better take my SUV."

"The truck's fine."

"The truck is a piece of junk." She laughed and for the first time in weeks actually felt human. Normal. Grabbing her keys from the counter by the door, she said, "Take the SUV."

He smiled as if hearing her laugh had been worth the insult to his beloved truck. But he glanced worriedly at her belly and set her keys on the counter again. "You can't drive the truck. It's a standard. If I take your car, you're stranded."

She pointed at the sky. "As if I'm going out in this."

"Right."

"So go."

Still, he hesitated.

Impatience crawled up her spine. She was tired, achy and just wanted to be alone. Specifically, she wanted a nice shower and two hours of mindless television so she could forget her backache, forget that she had another week of carrying this baby, forget that she and Nick weren't really a match.

He looked down at the keys, then back up at her. He studied her face for several seconds. "Okay. Fine. I'm going."

Though it was difficult, she mustered a smile.

He stepped out into the wind.

Grateful for the reprieve and knowing she had at least twenty minutes before the storm actually broke, she climbed the stairs, turned on the shower and stepped into the warm spray. Her back had ached all day. Her feet thumped with the weariness of having to support her burgeoning weight. But most of all her heart hurt.

She might have spent the day not looking for Nick, but now that she was alone, in the quiet, quiet house, she couldn't get him out of her mind. Losing Josh had been nothing compared to losing Nick. She should have known that. She should have realized that getting involved with the man who'd stolen her heart at six and let her leave him at eighteen, would end in the kind of heartbreak that tore through her soul, leaving tattered, unmendable pieces in its wake.

She forced her head under the spray as tears pooled in her eyes. She wasn't feeling sorry for herself. She was angry with herself. She'd been through this before. And though she'd been the one to leave Nick the first time, she'd always known she wasn't quite right for him. He was smart, strong, gorgeous. She had to force herself to do things, push herself to be bold. She wasn't even sure how to behave in the world he now lived in. And she certainly wasn't gorgeous.

Hell, today she looked more like a whale than a woman.

The tears in her eyes spilled over and ran down her cheeks. Again, she didn't try to stop them. Her entire body ached, but her broken heart shimmered with misery. Because she hurt so badly she decided not to fight it. She'd take this night and grieve the loss of her one true love, then tomorrow morning she'd be fine. There would be no more reason for her dad to worry about her. She'd pull herself together and no matter how intense the pain that sneaked up on her, no matter how lonely she'd get for the one person who'd ever made her genuinely happy, she would put on a smile and she would get through her life as if she were the luckiest, most blessed woman in the world.

Actually, once she had her baby she would be the luckiest, most blessed woman in the world. She'd have her dad. She'd have her baby. She would have the family she'd always longed for as a child but never quite fit into.

When she knew her skin would prune if she spent any more time under the spray of water, she hauled herself out and wrapped herself in a towel.

The first swipe of lightning raced across the sky. Were she in a better mood, she would have smiled at her timing. Instead she groaned when pain filled her back. This was awful. She'd known she'd be uncomfortable the last week of her pregnancy, but she hadn't expected this kind of torture.

Another flash of lightning streaked through the thick black clouds as she waddled to the bedroom. This was not looking good.

Still, what did she care? She had four hours till midnight. Four hours left in her self-declared night of mourning. She intended to use them.

But the next lightning bolt hit close. Her room filled with light, and a crack and boom immediately followed. She didn't even get seconds to count in between the lightning and the thunder. They were almost simultaneous, which meant the strike had been within a mile of her home.

The bedroom light flickered.

No. No. No! She could not lose the electricity. If she had to grieve in a dark house, she'd be beyond pathetic. Just let her keep the lights.

They flickered again then blinked off completely.

Light from the candles she'd left in the bathroom sent a wink of a glow into the hall. With a groan and a hand on her aching back, she made her way to the bathroom. She picked up the two scented candles she'd had sitting on the vanity and carried them back to her bedroom.

She really wasn't in the mood to wrestle into pajamas, so she drew a nightgown over her head. Her plan had been to make herself some hot cocoa, sit on the porch and cry. But the storm had brought a heavy humidity, making it too hot and humid for cocoa. The wind was too strong for her to sit on the porch. The lightning too close.

And as for crying, she could do that in her bedroom. On her bed.

She lay down. Suddenly the ache that had been in her back, raced around her sides to her tummy.

Dear God. What if she was in labor? A week early. With no car.

She settled herself. She'd simply call 9-1-1. It wasn't a big deal.

Except that her purse with her cell phone was downstairs and she now ached so badly she didn't think she could move.

Nick's lightweight shirt blew in the wind whipping across his deck that overlooked the ocean. Normally he loved to watch storms wreak havoc miles out over the water and wait for the resultant crash of the waves on his shore. But this storm was here. Any second now sheets of water would drench the happy little tourist town and anyone foolish enough to be standing on his deck.

Yet he didn't feel like going inside.

He ached so much he pressed his hand to his chest and rubbed the spot where he believed his heart to be.

Lightning streaked through the billowing black clouds, followed by a roar of thunder. Only an idiot tempted fate by making himself a target for lightning, no matter how awful he felt. He turned to go inside and found himself face-to-face with his brothers. Darius looked worried. Cade carried a case of beer.

His spirits lifted, and for the first time since discovering he wasn't the only Andreas son, he was abundantly glad he had siblings.

"Are we in a hurricane?"

Cade laughed at Darius. "Greenhorn, where I come from this isn't even a really big storm."

With his hands on both of his brothers' shoulders, Nick turned them and urged them inside. "This might not be a big storm where you come from but where you *are* it's a dilly. So move."

He closed the French doors behind them, two seconds before the first wave of rain hit. It pelted the glass like a million tiny diamonds. A continuous clicking sound filled his kitchen, as the lights flickered then went out.

"Great."

"Well, since there's no power for the refrigerator, it looks like we'll have to drink this beer."

Nick couldn't help it. He laughed. Cade was nothing if not pragmatic. A night with two stupid brothers was exactly what he needed to forget that he'd lost Maggie again. And this time it was his fault.

"Toss me a can."

"It's bottles. Walk over and get one."

Nick first went for the flashlight he kept in the top drawer of the cabinets. He hit the button and illuminated the room in an eerie beam of light.

Darius took a beer from Cade. "Too bad we can't sit outside and watch this."

"Yeah." Cade cast a longing glance out at the ocean. "That's some storm."

"Thought you were used to bigger?" Nick said, also accepting a beer from Cade.

"I am. But I'm also landlocked. I don't get to see anything like this on the water."

"We can go downstairs. Sit under the house."

Cade was already on his way to the stairs. "I forgot about that."

In two minutes, they were under the house, on rickety lawn chairs, drinking beer, watching the storm.

"I hope Maggie's not out in this."

And with those words from Darius, Nick suddenly realized why his brothers had come. He'd thought they'd noticed his apprehension when he'd left Andreas Holdings that afternoon. He had to be at the plant on Monday and he would see Maggie for the first time in six weeks. They knew he still hurt over her. They also knew he believed he'd made all the right choices. But he still hurt. And he still worried about seeing Maggie.

So he'd suspected they'd hopped on Cade's plane and followed him. To support him. But they weren't here for him. They were worried about Maggie.

"She's fine. She has her dad. Her friends. People at the plant took to her like bees to honey. She's got at least eight mother hens who fawn all over her."

Darius took a slug of beer. "She doesn't want her dad or a mother hen. According to Whitney, she's probably curled up in a ball of despair, wondering what the hell she did wrong."

"She didn't do anything."

Cade leaned around Darius and nudged Nick's arm. "Yeah. We get that part, genius."

"So, what? You're mad at me, too?"

"More like confused." Always calm and in control, Darius spoke with the air of authority. "You can't tell us that you don't love her. We see it on your sappy face. Yet you walked away when she needs you the most."

"She doesn't need me."

Cade barked a laugh. "Ah, poor, Nick. The love of his life doesn't need him."

"Shut up."

Darius turned to Cade. "Yeah, Cade. That's not helping."

Cade faced the ocean. "Okay. Fine. I'll just drink my beer and wait for waves to start splashing across our toes."

They were silent for a minute as the wind and rain, lightning and thunder put on a grand show.

Finally Nick said, "Power's probably going to be out all night." He sucked in a breath. "But Maggie's not alone." He told himself he'd only said that to alleviate his brothers' concerns. Not because a tiny spark of panic had welled up in his gut. "She's got her dad. And a car. And a cell phone."

"Right," Darius agreed. "She's probably fine."

"I mean…what could happen?" Nick took a quick drink of his beer, feeling odd tentacles of fear crawling up his spine with icy fingers. "She's due but not till next week." He sucked in a breath. "Though the last time I saw her she looked really big. So big that I'd wondered if she'd miscalculated her due date."

Darius groaned. "I hope you didn't tell her that."

He was digging, trying to get Nick to tell him about their fight, but horrible self-loathing and disappointment filled him. After the way they'd all taken to Gino, he'd never tell them. He couldn't tell them. They'd think him as crazy as Maggie did.

Instead he said, "I don't have a death wish."

Cade laughed, but much to Nick's relief didn't say anything.

Nick settled back in his chair. Rubbed his hand over the

day-old stubble of beard on his chin and cheeks. Maggie was fine. The power was out, but she was with her dad.

He squeezed his eyes shut. "Janette told me her dad has bereavement group every Friday night." Shooting out of his chair, he headed for the steps and his SUV keys. "She's alone in this."

He wasn't surprised that neither of his brothers argued when he bolted out into the night. He wasn't even surprised that he was going to check on her. He dialed her cell phone, but she didn't answer.

And suddenly he needed all his concentration for driving. Tree limbs had broken off. Water washed across the road. So he tossed his phone to the seat beside him and kept going.

He loved her. There'd never been any doubt in his mind that he loved her. He might be a fool who was so torn up about her baby that he couldn't accept him or her, but he'd never doubted his love for Maggie.

Ducking rain, he raced up the front porch steps to her house. He pounded on the door. "Maggie!"

She didn't answer. He tried several times and gave up. Though it wasn't late, she could be in bed, sleeping. And he was being foolish. So they were having a storm. She'd probably gone wherever she needed to go before it started. She might have driven her dad to bereavement group and decided to stay with him rather than ride home in the storm alone.

That was probably it.

Feeling foolish, he raced back to the SUV, accompanied by the roar of thunder, the pounding of the rain. His hand stalled above the door handle.

What if she was inside but just plain couldn't hear him?

What if she was afraid?

Lightning hit a nearby tree. Thunder roared like a hungry lion.

Hell, he was afraid.

He ran up the porch steps again, and, this time, tried the front door. It was unlocked. She wouldn't leave her house unlocked if she wasn't here.

He searched the downstairs first, calling her name. "Maggie! Maggie!"

But no answer.

He bolted upstairs, taking the steps two and three at a time as panic rolled through him.

Bursting into the room, he said only, "Maggie." She lay on the bed, curled up in a fetal position.

She turned to him. Tears streamed down her cheeks. Her eyes were glassy. "The baby's coming. I can't move. I couldn't even get to my cell phone."

Panic seized Nick. Trees and power lines were down. Even if she'd gotten to a phone, and called 9-1-1, there was no guarantee an ambulance could have gotten here.

He sat on the edge of the bed, trying to remember the books he'd read fifteen years before when she was pregnant with his child.

Sobbing, she said, "I'm so glad you came."

He blinked back his own tears. He was worthless. Ridiculously worthless. Always worthless when it came to Maggie.

He caught her hand. "I'm glad, too—"

She moaned suddenly and squeezed his hand. "Oh, God, Nick. This baby is coming right now."

Not giving himself time to think, he jumped up and grabbed the covers, tossing them off the bed.

She rolled to her back, her knees up, her legs spread, as if nature had taken over.

Which was good. He was going to need more than a

little help from Mother Nature, if they were going to get through this.

"Where are your scissors, towels and a basin for water?"

Grabbing her knees, she reared up and groaned through a pain that had to have been excruciating. "Towels are in the bathroom closet. Scissors are in the top drawer of the bathroom vanity. Basin is in the kitchen, beneath the sink."

"Okay. Hang on. I'll be back as soon as I can."

Taking one of her candles with him, he raced to the kitchen and found the basin. He flew back up the stairs, hurled himself into the bathroom and grabbed an armload of towels and the scissors.

When he returned to the room, Maggie was panting. Her gown had worked its way up her tummy.

Sweat beaded on Nick's forehead, but he didn't stop or take time to think. He grabbed two towels and slid them under her before taking the basin to the bathroom and filling it with hot water. While there, he grabbed some alcohol.

He pulled out his phone to call 9-1-1, hoping they'd reach the farm before the baby was born, but Maggie groaned.

"He's coming!"

Nick doused his hands in alcohol then rinsed them in the water before he raced to the foot of the bed. As she'd said, the baby was coming. He watched the head crown, then the shoulders ease through one at a time and caught the baby before it hit the bed. He grabbed another towel and wrapped the baby, laying him on Maggie's stomach so he could cut the cord.

Maggie's eyes filled with tears. "Oh, my God, Nick. It's a boy! Look at him. He's beautiful."

Nick paused. Actually looked at the baby. A boy. He swallowed. Tears filled his eyes. "He is beautiful."

"So tiny."

He glanced at the absolutely perfect miniature fingers and toes. An unexpected smile formed. "He's probably the smallest person I've ever seen."

Unnamed emotions skittered through him. He blamed it on coming down from the adrenaline that had spiked in his blood. After handling the rest of the birth, he washed his hands and called 9-1-1. He explained the situation to the dispatcher and she said she'd send an ambulance immediately.

When he disconnected the call, the silence in the room was deafening. He didn't know what to say. What to do. He'd known Maggie was in trouble and raced to her. But now that the trouble was over, they were still the same people.

She patted the bed beside her. "Sit."

He ambled over. Sat on the bed. Glanced at the baby. "He's so beautiful."

She smiled. "Yes. He is. Thank you. I don't know what would have happened without you."

His chest ached. He pictured her on the bed, alone, scared, not able to handle the situation for herself. Still, he said, "You would have been fine. It was a very easy delivery."

She gaped at him. "Do you not get it yet? Nick, I need you. Everybody needs somebody sometime and every time I've really needed somebody you have been there."

He smiled reluctantly. "Sort of like fate."

"Sort of like destiny."

He looked at the baby again. So tiny. So perfect. Then he glanced at Maggie. So content. So perfect. "I can be an ass."

"Or maybe it just takes you a while to think things through and come to terms with it all."

Wrapping his fingers around the baby's middle, he lifted the towel-clad bundle from Maggie's tummy. "Welcome to the world, kid."

Maggie laughed.

"My God. I thought Gino was small when we got him at six months. This kid is like one-tenth his size." He caught her gaze. "He really needs us."

"Yes, he does." She smiled slowly. "And I really need you."

The joy of hearing that enveloped his heart, warmed it enough that he could take a risk. "I need you, too."

She caught his fingers and squeezed. "I'm so sorry I got angry that you were afraid you couldn't love him."

"Shh. It's fine. We're fine." He glanced at the baby. "Maybe better than fine. My God. He's so adorable. I can't believe I was afraid."

"I can understand. I—"

"No, Maggie. I was jealous." He closed his eyes in misery. "My brothers and I made a pact when we decided to become brothers for real. No secrets. So no secrets here, either. I was jealous." He swallowed. "You had lost our baby. Another man had given you this child...this child that you'd get a chance to hold and love. I couldn't get past that."

"Nick—" His name whispered to him as she slid her hand across his. "Have you ever really grieved our baby?"

He sucked in a breath. "I'm not sure."

"You need to do that. You need to let yourself feel all the pain of his loss and put him in a special place in your heart."

"I wonder what he would have looked like."

"Well, seeing how the Andreas genes seem to dominate, I'd guess he'd have been dark-haired with dark eyes."

Nick smiled.

"And a devil. Ornery, but fun."

This time Nick laughed. "Yeah. That's how I saw him, too."

"So keep him in your heart."

He swallowed hard and nodded.

"And take care of me and Egbert."

His head snapped up. "Egbert?"

"Sure. It's an old family name that no one's used in decades."

He rose, rocking the brand-new baby boy. "There's a reason it hasn't been used in decades. As names go, it sucks."

She laughed.

The noise of the ambulance pulling into the farm rolled into the room a few seconds before red and blue lights flashed through.

"So, you don't like Egbert. What do you think we should name him?"

He looked down, love filled his heart until he thought his chest would explode from it.

He caught her gaze. "Michael Nicholas Andreas."

She smiled. "That's a great name."

"He's a great kid."

"He is."

He paced to the window, saw the ambulance crew getting out and faced her again. "And you'll marry me."

"Well, I'll have to if you're adopting my son and giving him your last name."

He laughed. The ambulance crew hustled in. Took the baby. Cared for Maggie.

And Nick leaned against the windowsill. For fifteen years he'd cursed fate. Now suddenly he didn't hate the old bat so much. He had Maggie back. For real. For good.

And he had a son.

EPILOGUE

WHITNEY and Darius had insisted on bringing Gino to North Carolina for the baptism. While the waters had become too cold to swim in New York, the beach in North Carolina was still warm and sunny.

Still, they'd held the baptism dinner at Maggie's dad's house. *He'd* insisted.

"All right. All right," Charlie yelled, calming the noisy group. He'd gotten out Vicki's good china and her crystal for wine and set the big table in the formal dining room. "Turkey will be carved in about two minutes. There's no reason to get restless."

Gino yelped, pointing at the mashed potatoes and gravy on Whitney's plate.

"Yes, they're yours," Whitney said with a laugh.

"What's his?"

All eyes turned toward the arched entryway, when Cade walked in.

Maggie was about to jump up and give him a hug since he'd said he wouldn't be able to make it, but Nick said, "You missed the actual baptism."

He strolled to a seat at the table. "Had to fly myself over," he said, pulling out a chair and straddling it. "Can't fly in a suit, can't go to church in jeans."

Charlie harrumphed. "Lots of people go to church in jeans."

"That's just an excuse," Whitney said, handing him a plate and some silver.

Darius shook his head. "I just think he's so accustomed to being with cattle that he sometimes forgets how to be human."

Cade threw a fresh dinner roll at him. "At least I'm not so pampered that I use bath salts."

Whitney gaped. "Bath salts are good for the skin."

And so it went. Charlie passed out slices of juicy turkey. Nick, Cade and Darius teased. Gino ate his mashed potatoes. Maggie and Whitney talked about caring for infants as Maggie cuddled her newborn baby.

Things weren't perfect. But life rarely was. But, finally, finally, she had a family. The family she'd always longed for. The family Nick had promised at eighteen that he would give her.

Coming Next Month

Available June 14, 2011

You can find more information on upcoming
Harlequin® titles, free excerpts and more at
www.HarlequinInsideRomance.com.

HRCNM0511

REQUEST YOUR FREE BOOKS!
2 FREE NOVELS PLUS 2 FREE GIFTS!

Harlequin

Romance

From the Heart, For the Heart

YES! Please send me 2 FREE Harlequin® Romance novels and my 2 FREE gifts (gifts are worth about $10). After receiving them, if I don't wish to receive any more books, I can return the shipping statement marked "cancel". If I don't cancel, I will receive 6 brand-new novels every month and be billed just $3.84 per book in the U.S. or $4.24 per book in Canada. That's a savings of at least 15% off the cover price! It's quite a bargain! Shipping and handling is just 50¢ per book in the U.S. and 75¢ per book in Canada.* I understand that accepting the 2 free books and gifts places me under no obligation to buy anything. I can always return a shipment and cancel at any time. Even if I never buy another book, the two free books and gifts are mine to keep forever.

116/316 HDN FC6H

Name	(PLEASE PRINT)	
Address		Apt. #
City	State/Prov.	Zip/Postal Code

Signature (if under 18, a parent or guardian must sign)

Mail to the **Reader Service:**
IN U.S.A.: P.O. Box 1867, Buffalo, NY 14240-1867
IN CANADA: P.O. Box 609, Fort Erie, Ontario L2A 5X3

Not valid for current subscribers to Harlequin Romance books.

**Are you a subscriber to Harlequin Romance books
and want to receive the larger-print edition?
Call 1-800-873-8635 or visit www.ReaderService.com.**

* Terms and prices subject to change without notice. Prices do not include applicable taxes. Sales tax applicable in N.Y. Canadian residents will be charged applicable taxes. Offer not valid in Quebec. This offer is limited to one order per household. All orders subject to credit approval. Credit or debit balances in a customer's account(s) may be offset by any other outstanding balance owed by or to the customer. Please allow 4 to 6 weeks for delivery. Offer available while quantities last.

Your Privacy—The Reader Service is committed to protecting your privacy. Our Privacy Policy is available online at www.ReaderService.com or upon request from the Reader Service.

We make a portion of our mailing list available to reputable third parties that offer products we believe may interest you. If you prefer that we not exchange your name with third parties, or if you wish to clarify or modify your communication preferences, please visit us at www.ReaderService.com/consumerchoice or write to us at Reader Service Preference Service, P.O. Box 9062, Buffalo, NY 14269. Include your complete name and address.

HRI1

Harlequin® Blaze™ brings you
New York Times *and* USA TODAY *bestselling author*
Vicki Lewis Thompson with three new steamy titles
from the bestselling miniseries SONS OF CHANCE

Chance isn't just the last name of these rugged
Wyoming cowboys—it's their motto, too!

Read on for a sneak peek at the first title,
SHOULD'VE BEEN A COWBOY

Available June 2011 only from Harlequin® Blaze™.

"THANKS FOR NOT TURNING ON THE LIGHTS," Tyler said. "I'm a mess."

"Not in my book." Even in low light, Alex had a good view of her yellow shirt plastered to her body. It was all he could do not to reach for her, mud and all. But the next move needed to be hers, not his.

She slicked her wet hair back and squeezed some water out of the ends as she glanced upward. "I like the sound of the rain on a tin roof."

"Me, too."

She met his gaze briefly and looked away. "Where's the sink?"

"At the far end, beyond the last stall."

Tyler's running shoes squished as she walked down the aisle between the rows of stalls. She glanced sideways at Alex. "So how much of a cowboy are you these days? Do you ride the range and stuff?"

"I ride." He liked being able to say that. "Why?"

"Just wondered. Last summer, you were still a city boy. You even told me you weren't the cowboy type, but you're...different now."

He wasn't sure if that was a good thing or a bad thing. Maybe she preferred city boys to cowboys. "How am I different?"

"Well, you dress differently, and your hair's a little longer. Your face seems a little more chiseled, but maybe that's because of your hair. Also, there's something else, something harder to define, an attitude…"

"Are you saying I have an attitude?"

"Not in a bad way. It's more like a quiet confidence."

He was flattered, but still he had to laugh. "I just admitted a while ago that I have all kinds of doubts about this event tomorrow. That doesn't seem like quiet confidence to me."

"This isn't about your job, it's about…your…" She took a deep breath. "It's about your sex appeal, okay? I have no business talking about it, because it will only make me want to do things I shouldn't do." She started toward the end of the barn. "Now, where's that sink? We need to get cleaned up and go back to the house. Dinner is probably ready, and I—"

He spun her around and pulled her into his arms, mud and all. "Let's do those things." Then he kissed her, knowing that she would kiss him back, knowing that this time he would take that kiss where he wanted it to go. And she would let him.

Follow Tyler and Alex's wild adventures in
SHOULD'VE BEEN A COWBOY
Available June 2011 only from Harlequin® Blaze™
wherever books are sold.

SPECIAL EDITION

Life, Love and Family

LOVE CAN BE FOUND IN THE MOST UNLIKELY PLACES, ESPECIALLY WHEN YOU'RE NOT LOOKING FOR IT...

Failed marriages, broken families and disappointment. Cecilia and Brandon have both been unlucky in love and life and are ripe for an intervention. Good thing Brandon's mother happens to stumble upon this matchmaking project. But will Brandon be able to open his eyes and get away from his busy career to see that all he needs is right there in front of him?

FIND OUT IN

WHAT THE SINGLE DAD WANTS...

BY *USA TODAY* BESTSELLING AUTHOR

MARIE FERRARELLA

AVAILABLE IN JUNE 2011
WHEREVER BOOKS ARE SOLD.